SHATTERED TRUST

ESTELLE WETHERBY

CONTENTS

PART 1 - LOVE TOKEN

Hey, Artsy Diary,

I'm back after a while. Life's been chaotic, but that's no excuse. You've always been a place of solace for me, like an old friend waiting patiently for me to return.

The scent of these pages brings back memories—does it for you, too? It reminds me of the time I first held his letter.

It was the scent that lingered the longest, a mix of vanilla and something sweeter. The envelope was creased from its journey, but inside, his words danced across the paper. And what did I ask for? Just something small, a gesture. But he sent a song. A whole song. I don't think I could have asked for more.

It wasn't just the song, though. No, it was the photograph he sent along with it. Those eyes, they captured everything, didn't they? But the lips—how do I even begin to describe them? Am I being too forward? Probably. But when you've known someone for so long, it's hard to hold back. His smile, that same smile that made everything feel lighter, still brightens my memories of him. Even though life has taken us down separate roads, I'm genuinely happy for him. He deserves all the happiness in the world.

I can still remember the melody of the song. It echoed in my mind long after I read the note. I sang it out loud once, hoping that, somewhere, he was singing it too. His voice would have made it a lullaby, a song that could calm even the most restless of hearts.

"Teardrops fall on the notes while writing."

Not because we weren't meant to be together, but because I lacked the strength to fight for what we had. Now, with miles between us—emotional, and geographical—it feels like a gulf that I'll never be able to cross.

I clicked my pen and let my thoughts drift.

People are sweet until they stop expressing themselves. Isn't it odd? We, as humans, are given this unique ability to communicate, yet, more often than not, we let that gift fall by the wayside. I see it all the time in the world around me. Even animals have a way of sharing their emotions, though they can't use words like we do.

Just then, the window shutter rattled. Startled, I stood up and moved to close it. I was about to latch it shut when I saw two birds, chirping together on a branch nearby. They seemed so carefree, so lost in their own world, and I couldn't bring myself to close the window just yet. As I turned back to my room, my eyes caught sight of a house across the street. It was wrapped in a garland of fresh flowers, each one cascading down from the roof like they were placed by a loving hand. It looked like something out of a storybook.

"Daisy! Daisy!"

My mom's voice rang out from downstairs, snapping me from my reverie. I quickly made my way down, only to stub my toe on the last step. "AH... AMMA!" I yelped, clutching my foot. My dad rushed over, concern etched on his face.

"What happened? Are you okay?"

I winced. "Just a bad stair," I muttered, forcing a smile through the pain. "Mom, why did you call me?"

"Oh, I just wanted to show you a lily that bloomed in the garden."

"Seriously, Mom? You called me down for that?" I grumbled, rubbing my foot.

"I was excited, Daisy," she said with a sheepish smile.

Dad laughed. "Your mom could make anything sound like breaking news. So dramatic."

Mom shot him a look that could've cut through stone. It was her silent way of saying, "You'll be cooking dinner tonight". I smirked, limping back upstairs. I sank into my rocking chair and plugged in my earphones, needing a moment to myself.

In seventh grade, I had a sleek pen box where dreams met paper. By eighth grade, I carried a keychain with my name engraved on a single grain of rice—my tiny symbol of hope and rising dreams. Ninth grade brought a bracelet, glittering brightly, spelling out "Happy Friendship Day." By tenth grade, a glass teddy bear sat on my shelf, reflecting the innocent love we shared. And in eleventh grade, I wore a watch, its steady ticking a reminder that time, like our dreams, was always in motion.

Those were the gifts that marked our journey, tokens of the words we shared, the sleepless nights, the promises, and, eventually, the distance that we couldn't cross. How does it feel to stand at a crossroads, knowing that the light you once followed now illuminates a path you can no longer walk?

The thought makes me shudder, but there's no turning back now.

I got up from my chair and approached the mirror on the wall. It's not just any mirror—it's magical. The frame is intricately carved with elephants and flowers, like a portal into a forgotten world. I looked at my reflection, tired from the weight of the evening, the twilight shadows clinging to my skin. My face was a poem waiting for the right poet to discover it.

But there's no Flynn Rider here to brush away the stray strand of hair that falls across my face—no handwritten letters with the scent of roses. The only bouquets I've received are digital, fleeting, and unreal.

Part 2 - MIA (Missing In Action)

irrors have a strange way of pulling you in. Sometimes it feels like you're looking for something—some flicker of familiarity, something that might make sense of the person staring back at you. I remember hating my nose. A friend once compared it to an elephant's trunk, and from that day on, I felt like I didn't belong. It was as if the reflection in the mirror was a stranger, a constant reminder of all my insecurities. I felt like an alien in my own body, lost in a world that didn't seem to want me.

But then he came along, with his crooked smile and his way of turning the world on its head. He saw beauty where I saw flaws. He said my nose reminded him of a parrot's beak, and for some reason, that made me laugh. His lightheartedness broke through the walls I had built around myself, and suddenly, I felt seen. He made me proud of what I had once hated, and in his presence, I started to embrace the very things I had tried so hard to hide.

As I sat on my bed that morning, the weight of everything pressing down on me, I untied my braids, running my fingers through my hair. I sprayed dry shampoo to freshen it up, the familiar scent providing a momentary comfort.

My sunflower claw clip lay on the dresser, a little treasure I'd found in a small store downtown, and as I picked it up, memories flooded back of lazy afternoons spent wandering through shops, sharing dreams and laughter.

I pinned up my hair, the bright yellow clip standing out against my dark strands like a beacon of hope amidst the chaos.

Dressing was an act of defiance against the heaviness in my heart. I slipped into my favorite blue frock, adorned with red flowers, the fabric soft and worn from years of wear. Each thread carried echoes of happier days—days spent dreaming of the future, with him by my side. I clasped the bracelet he had given me around my wrist. It still glimmered in the morning light, a reminder of the bond we shared, and I felt a flicker of strength, though it was quickly overshadowed by the uncertainty that loomed over me.

Downstairs, my parents were glued to the news, their faces pale and drawn.

The headline flashed across the screen—Police, a Search, Someone Missing.

My heart raced, but I didn't think much of it, just kissed them goodbye and left on my bike, the weight of their worry trailing behind me like a shadow.

The library has always been my refuge, the one place where everything feels quiet, even when my mind is a chaotic storm. I could lose myself among the pages of books, escape into worlds far removed from my own.

But today, as I walked in, something felt disturbingly wrong. His face—his face was everywhere. Posters plastered on walls, flyers strewn across the front desk, his name written in bold black letters, with a single word underneath: MISSING.

My heart dropped into the pit of my stomach. I stood frozen in the doorway, my breath catching in my throat, the world around me fading to a dull blur. The room seemed to close in around me, the air thick with unspoken fear.

I could hear murmurs from the police officers near the entrance, their voices low but urgent, like the distant hum of bees in a garden now shrouded in shadows. They were piecing together the puzzle of his disappearance, their expressions grim, their brows furrowed with concern.

"What happened?" I finally managed to ask, my voice barely above a whisper, as if speaking louder would shatter the fragile atmosphere.

One of the officers turned to me, his expression somber and weary. "He's been missing for the last four days," he said, the weight of his words settling heavily in the air.

"No leads, no clues. Just... gone."

The ground felt like it had been pulled out from under me. A sense of vertigo swept over me as I stumbled outside, barely able to breathe. The sunlight felt harsh, biting at my skin, illuminating the reality I was desperate to deny. Panic surged through me, a tidal wave of fear crashing against the walls of my mind. My legs moved on instinct as I made my way to Theo's house, hoping—praying—that he would have answers. Theo had always been his closest friend. He'd know something, anything.

When I reached Theo's door, I knocked frantically, my heart racing. After what felt like an eternity, he opened the door. His face was pale and drawn, dark circles under his eyes revealing sleepless nights and haunting thoughts.

"Daisy..." he began, his voice strained, heavy with guilt and sorrow. "I don't know what happened. He called me the night before he disappeared, asking me to go with him to the waterfall. But I couldn't go. I had paperwork for my dad's land. And now... now I regret it. I should've gone. I should've been there."

His words hung in the air like a weight neither of us could lift, the unspoken accusation sharp between us. I could feel the tension tightening like a noose, pulling us both into the depths of despair. "You didn't know," I murmured, though deep down, I felt the prick of accusation. What if he had gone? What if he could have saved him?

"I could have," Theo replied, anguish twisting his face. "If I had just gone with him..."

A heavy silence enveloped us, thick with guilt and regret. My mind raced, trying to process everything. "What do we do now?" I asked, my voice trembling.

"We have to find out what happened," he said, determination sparking in his eyes. "We can't just sit here and do nothing."

As we stood there, I felt the weight of his gaze upon me, a mix of expectation and desperation. We were at a crossroads, both haunted by the echoes of our choices. What if we were too late? What if we couldn't find him? I swallowed hard, forcing myself to look into his eyes. I could see the fear mirrored in his expression, and it sent chills down my spine.

"Okay," I said finally, steeling myself against the impending dread. "Let's figure this out."

But as the words left my mouth, a strange sensation washed over me, a feeling of foreboding that wrapped around my chest like a vice. I hesitated, glancing back at my bike, then at the ground, where the shadows began to lengthen. The thought of heading to the waterfall filled me with dread. I couldn't shake the feeling that we might be walking into something dangerous—something I wasn't ready to face.

"Wait," I said, my voice quaking. "Maybe... maybe we shouldn't go right now."

Theo frowned, confusion flickering across his features. "What do you mean? We need to—"

"I just... I don't think I can handle it. Not like this. What if we don't find anything? What if it's worse than we think?" My heart raced as I spoke, fear creeping in like a shadow.

Theo studied me for a moment, his eyes searching mine for answers. Finally, he nodded, though his expression was heavy with disappointment. "Alright. We can wait. But we need to figure this out, Daisy. We can't let fear stop us."

I forced a smile, though it felt strained and brittle. "I know. I just need a little time."

I could no longer ignore the gnawing feeling that my life was unraveling, that something sinister lay just beyond my reach, waiting for the perfect moment to strike.

PART 3 - TASTE OF MYSTERY

After talking with Theo, the weight of his words hit me like a punch to the gut. My mind reeled, too shocked to form coherent thoughts. I tried to say something—anything—but the words lodged in my throat. So instead, I hugged him tightly, whispering the only words I could muster.

"He'll be back soon... he has to," I murmured into his shoulder, my voice trembling with uncertainty. I could feel Theo's body tense, the same fear rippling through both of us.

Reluctantly, I pulled away, offering him a weak smile, though I knew it didn't reach my eyes. "I'll see you later, Theo," I said softly, trying to sound more confident than I felt. He just nodded, his gaze hollow.

As I rode home, my mind churned in a storm of conflicting emotions. I felt trapped between two worlds: one where everything still felt whole, and another where everything was unraveling. Was he safe? Was he even alive? The unspoken questions gnawed at me, twisting my stomach in knots.

Suddenly, the sky opened up without warning. Sheets of rain pelted the ground, drenching me in seconds. The storm came out of nowhere, wild and unrelenting. I spotted a bar up ahead and made a beeline for it, desperately seeking shelter.

The moment I stepped inside, the warmth wrapped around me like a blanket, but my soaked clothes clung to me uncomfortably. I dashed to the restroom, shivering, hoping to dry off under the air hand dryer.

Inside, a group of girls crowded the mirror, oblivious to the storm raging outside. They were perfectly made up—hair styled, makeup flawless—laughing as they playfully kissed their reflections, leaving lipstick stains on the glass. I watched them, a strange mix of envy and amusement bubbling inside me. Their carefree energy was so far from where my head was. They giggled as they tossed me friendly, exaggerated flying kisses, and for a moment, their tipsy camaraderie lifted my spirits.

There's something magical about women bonding in bar restrooms. It's like we become instant friends, sharing compliments and laughter, even if we never learn each other's names. It made me feel a little less alone, at least for a moment.

I left the restroom and slid onto a stool at the bar, ordering a glass of water. As I gulped it down, a shiver raced down my spine—not from the cold, but from something else. I felt it before I saw him, the warm breath grazing the back of my neck. My body stiffened, alert to the unfamiliar presence so close behind me.

A soft, almost deliberate touch followed—a drink placed gently in front of me. My heart skipped a beat as I sensed the quiet confidence in the gesture. I turned my head just enough to catch a glimpse of his hand, resting on the bar beside me. It was strong and graceful, the veins faintly visible under his skin, radiating a kind of magnetism that drew me in.

For a brief, suspended moment, it felt like the entire bar faded away. The music, the chatter, even the rain outside—all of it became background noise, leaving only the charged space between us. I inhaled sharply, the scent of his cologne wrapping around me, subtle yet intoxicating.

"Negroni, please," he said. His voice—a low, velvety murmur—slipped through the air like a secret meant only for me. It sent a jolt of electricity through my veins, a strange thrill that left me breathless.

Before I could even think to respond, I felt something drape over my shoulders—his jacket. Its warmth cocooned me, a silent acknowledgment of the chill still clinging to my damp skin. I turned to thank him, but in the same instant, he was gone. Vanished into the crowd, leaving me with nothing but the lingering warmth of his presence.

I scanned the room desperately, hoping to catch another glimpse of him—his face, his eyes—anything that could anchor this fleeting encounter. But he was nowhere to be found. All I had were the echoes of his voice and the ghostly touch of his hand on my skin.

The clock on my phone flashed 11:33PM, pulling me back to reality with a jolt. I glanced down, realizing I had missed several calls from my parents. Guilt twisted in my gut. I'd left my phone on silent during my time at the library, and now I was paying for it.

Frantically, I dialed Dad's number. When he picked up, his voice was thick with worry.

"Where have you been? Why weren't you answering your phone?"

"I'm so sorry, Dad," I stammered. "I didn't hear it—it's been raining hard, and I got caught up. I'm heading home now."

His sigh on the other end of the line told me everything. "Just get home safely," he said, the worry still palpable in his voice.

As I hung up, the reality of the night settled heavily on my shoulders. The rain still pounded outside, mirroring the turmoil within me. I had to get home, but part of me was still tethered to that brief encounter in the bar—the stranger with the velvet voice, the jacket that still clung to my skin.

Part 4 – The Distance We Carry

The rain was still falling when I stumbled through the front door, the cold dampness clinging to my skin. My father's voice greeted me, sharp with concern.

"How could you be so careless? Not checking your phone, not telling us where you were?" His words sliced through the air, heavy with the weight of worry.

My mother stood beside him, her arms crossed. Though she said nothing, her silence spoke louder than any words she could've uttered. It felt like a wall between us, built from their unspoken fears and the storm of emotions that had followed me home.

"I'm sorry," I whispered, my voice small and strained.

"I didn't mean to worry you. It won't happen again."

The apology tasted hollow in my mouth, sinking like a stone in the tense quiet of the room. Their concern pressed down on me like a physical weight, a burden I couldn't shake off.

Without waiting for a response, I dragged myself upstairs, the exhaustion of the day finally catching up with me. Each step felt heavier than the last, like I was carrying the weight of all the moments I couldn't change. I collapsed onto my bed, staring blankly at the ceiling, feeling the chaos of the day churn inside me like a storm that refused to pass.

The city outside hummed with life—cars honking, people shouting, a distant echo of everything that kept moving forward, even when I felt like I couldn't.

I closed my eyes, willing the memories of the day to fade, but they replayed themselves like a film reel, over and over in my mind. His face—the man at the bar—flashed before me, a mystery wrapped in warmth and fleeting comfort. And then there was him—the one who was missing—his absence still gnawing at the edges of my thoughts, a wound I couldn't stop prodding.

Somewhere in the haze of exhaustion, I drifted off, my dreams a patchwork of voices and images that didn't quite fit together. I woke to the shrill sound of my alarm, groggy and disoriented, unsure of when I had even fallen asleep.

As I fumbled to silence the alarm, his voice drifted into my thoughts, faint yet clear: "You look cute in that dress." It was something he had once said, a memory tied to a playful moment shared over Snapchat maps and Bitmoji smiles. We used to trace the distance between us, mapping out every mile like explorers charting a course through unfamiliar seas.

I picked up my artsy diary from the floor, its pages worn and stained from too many nights spent pouring my heart onto paper. I tried to write, but the words wouldn't come. All I could think about was his voice, echoing in the space between us, growing fainter with each passing day.

The weight of it—the distance, the silence—felt suffocating. He never quite understood why I struggled to communicate the way he wanted. He used to say, "Communication builds bonds, but silence tears them apart," as if every unspoken word was another thread unraveling us.

In his eyes, my silence was a refusal—a choice to keep him at arm's length. But what he couldn't see was the war I waged within myself. For me, every conversation felt like walking a tightrope over my deepest fears. I wanted to reach out, to share every thought, every feeling, but something always held me back. The words that came so easily to him felt tangled inside me, knotted by the weight of my own uncertainties—and my parents' scrutiny.

He didn't know the full story. He couldn't. My parents watched me closely, always wondering who I was talking to, what I was hiding. They'd already suspected too much, and I couldn't risk them knowing the truth about us. Every message I sent, every phone call I made was a risk I wasn't sure I could afford. I'd learned to be careful—deleting our texts, clearing any trace of our conversations—because the fear of being caught loomed larger than the comfort of sharing my heart.

He believed that if we just talked more, everything would fall back into place, that the gaps between us could be filled with words. But what he saw as a simple solution—a bridge built from conversations—felt, to me, like an impossible distance. "Why don't you ever tell me what's on your mind?" he'd ask, his frustration clear, the hurt in his eyes unmistakable.

It wasn't that I didn't want to. I just... couldn't. My parents were always there, watching, and questioning. Every time I tried to open up, it felt like I was exposing a part of myself not only to him but to them as well. And that terrified me. I couldn't let them know how deep my feelings went, how much of my heart was tied to him.

He believed communication could save us, but for me, it wasn't that simple. I was trapped—between wanting to let him in and needing to keep him hidden from a world that wouldn't understand. And in the end, my silence spoke louder than I ever could.

"All Lies, he said,

All Love of Losing, I replied."

But tonight, with the rain pattering softly against my window, the fear seemed to quiet, replaced by something else—hope. I picked up my pen and began to write, not about the sorrow or the distance, but about the moments we had shared, the laughter, the connection that still flickered between us like a fading light.

Perhaps tomorrow would bring a chance to bridge the gap, to reach out and feel close again, even if only for a moment. I didn't know what the future held, but as I closed my diary, I let myself believe that somehow, in some way, we would find our way back to each other.

The rain continued to fall, a steady rhythm against the window, and as I drifted back into sleep, I whispered a silent wish to the stars beyond the clouds: for him to come back, for the distance to disappear, for us to feel whole again.

Part 5- Whispers of a Withered Dream

My hands trembled, each quiver sending shockwaves through my body. Tears blurred my vision, and sweat clung to my skin, wrapping me in a suffocating embrace. I felt paralyzed, as if my limbs were tethered to an invisible force, unable to escape the rising tide of dread. Deep, ragged breaths escaped my lips; I wasn't running, just lying there, yet my body was caught in a tempest of panic.

In that moment of clarity, I recognized the familiar grip of a panic attack—the second one in my life. The first had struck the day we broke up, and I had hoped never to face this darkness again. But here it was, crashing down like an unrelenting wave, dragging me under.

Memories flooded back—those nights spent tossing and turning, haunted by ghosts of sleeplessness. Each moment replayed in vivid detail: his laughter, the way his eyes sparkled when he talked about his dreams, and the final, stinging silence that lingered after our last conversation. I felt trapped in a nightmare that refused to release me.

Desperate to ground myself, I wrestled off the suffocating blanket, heat enveloping me like a vise. I reached for my phone, fumbling in the dark to check the time.

3:39 AM.

"Not this again," I groaned, the weight of déjà vu heavy on my chest. The first panic attack had left me sleepless for a month, each day a disorienting blur that dragged me deeper into despair, where shadows danced in the corners of my room, whispering fears that twisted around my mind like tendrils of smoke.

With shaking fingers, I opened the Hike Messenger app, the one I hadn't touched in ages. I had to unlock it first. The password had slipped my mind, so I quickly jotted it down in my notes: "White House."

I chuckled softly. It was absurdly cute and cringe-worthy. Our love had always been painted in colors—his "green house" password a reflection of the innocence we once shared. Silly, yes, but people do the most endearing things when they're in love. Those small acts made the heart ache the most after separation.

As I scrolled through the saved texts, a mix of nostalgia and regret washed over me. I realized my mistake: I never deleted them. Instead, I would block him. How terribly flawed that I hoarded both the sweet and bitter memories, saving snippets of our once-vibrant connection like artifacts of a long-lost civilization. I would block him when the pain became too much, yet the remnants of our conversations lingered, haunting me like an unfinished melody.

Some texts were one-sided, echoing his pleas for connection. Others were filled with my own frustration. "I can't do this again," I would reply, leaving him on read, my heart heavy with guilt. I felt like a terrible person, unable to grasp his point of view. He begged for communication, but I retreated into silence, each message an unyielding reminder of my weakness.

We had envisioned a future together, dreaming of a home filled with laughter—two workspaces where our ambitions could flourish side by side, walls adorned with memories of our shared adventures. But now, those dreams felt like a hollow echo, a reminder of all that had slipped away. The realization stung like a fresh wound, raw and bleeding.

Suddenly, the faint sound of laughter drifted from the street below, pulling me from my reverie. It was a group of friends, carefree and full of life, their voices rising like music in the night. My heart ached for the joy I once knew, moments filled with silly dances and whispered secrets. I remembered how he used to say, "We'll make our own music, you and I."

With a shuddering breath, I threw my phone aside, desperate to escape the spiraling thoughts that threatened to drown me. I stood up, my legs shaky as I navigated the stairs to grab some ice-cold eye patches. My eyes burned with unshed tears, and the cool sensation would offer a brief reprieve from the heat of emotion surging through me.

I stepped outside through the side door, seeking solace in the crisp night air. There, I noticed the tree we once admired, its branches reaching skyward, grown taller and stronger. When had it become so majestic? I remembered a summer day when we carved our initials into its trunk, a promise that felt unbreakable back then.

As the memory washed over me, I recalled the day he climbed over my balcony, his eyes filled with longing as he asked to see me. We had spent hours beneath that tree, whispering dreams and daring the universe to let them come true. "One day," he had said, "this tree will grow big enough to hide us from the world."

But now, standing beneath its sprawling branches, I felt the weight of our lost paths. The older we grew, the further apart we drifted. I wished we could reclaim the dreams we had spun together, but the reality was that those dreams had withered, leaving behind an emptiness that echoed in my heart.

As the tears flowed freely now, I closed my eyes and let the night air wash over me. The stars above were hidden behind clouds, much like our hopes buried in silence. It felt like a cruel joke that the tree thrived while our love lay dormant. I longed for him to understand the tangled mess of my heart—a heart still filled with echoes of laughter, dreams, and a love that was once unbreakable.

PART 6 - WOVEN MEMORIES

With a heavy heart, I turned away from the tree, the cool night air a bittersweet reminder of hat once was. The laughter from the street faded as I made my way back inside, the door creaking softly behind me. Each step felt like wading through thick mud, as if the weight of my memories pulled me down.

Once back in my room, I collapsed onto my bed, the soft sheets embracing me like a long-lost friend. I buried my face in the pillow, letting out a muffled sob, my body shaking with the force of unspoken grief. The familiar scent of lavender drifted from the fabric, a scent we used to share during late-night talks. It was a cruel reminder of all the moments we could have created, yet never would.

As I lay there, the darkness swallowed me whole, wrapping me in a cocoon of isolation. The only sounds were the soft ticking of the clock and the distant hum of cars passing by, an echo of life continuing without me. My heart raced, each beat resonating with memories of us: the day he surprised me with that beautiful dress, a deep shade of emerald that flowed like a river of silk. I could still remember the way he had grinned, his eyes sparkling with joy, as he said it reminded him of the color of the leaves in our favorite park.

"I can't wait to see you in it," he had said, his voice filled with anticipation. I could picture it perfectly—how it hugged my figure just right, flowing down to my knees and swirling around me as I twirled in front of the mirror, the fabric catching the light. It was a simple gift, yet it held the weight of so many unspoken promises. I wore it during our fleeting moments together, and each time I slipped it on, I felt like I was wearing a piece of our love.

Those rare moments we spent together outside the confines of our phones felt like stolen treasures. We didn't have many shared experiences in the physical world, but the few we had sparkled brightly: the spontaneous road trip that went longer than we had planned, laughter spilling over as we got lost, and the way we discovered that little mall with the cozy café where we shared our favorite food. The time I wore that dress to the mall, his hand resting on my back as we walked, felt like a scene plucked from a dream. The thrill of it all—walking side by side, just two kids in love—was a feeling I craved now more than ever.

But those days felt like fairy tales now—stories that belonged to someone else. I felt like a ghost in my own life, wandering through a house filled with echoes of a love that had turned to ashes. I clutched my phone, scrolling through our old photos, each image a vivid reminder of joy and heartache intertwined.

Then I stumbled upon a video: me wearing the dress, standing in a sunlit park, the wind tugging playfully at the fabric as I laughed at something he had said just off-camera. His laughter followed, a melody that danced in the air, and I couldn't help but smile through my tears, the memory washing over me like a warm tide. But just as quickly, the smile faded.

"I can't go back to that," I whispered to the silence, frustration creeping into my voice. The weight of reality crashed down again, and I felt the familiar panic bubbling up inside me. I pressed my hands to my chest, willing my heart to calm, but the fear spiraled as images of my parents' disappointed faces flashed in my mind.

love is messy.

Love is wild and unpredictable, like a storm that sweeps you off your feet and leaves you breathless.

I longed to share that whirlwind with them, to let them in on the secret joy and pain, but fear gripped my throat, suffocating me.

A sudden wave of realization crashed over me. I was suffocating under the weight of expectations—not just from my parents, but from myself. The fear of judgment, the fear of being misunderstood, it all pressed heavily on my chest. I felt trapped between two worlds: the one where I could be free and honest and the one where I had to wear a mask, pretending that everything was fine.

I rolled onto my back, staring at the ceiling, the shadows dancing above me like specters of my past. My heart raced, and I felt the familiar tightening in my chest. Panic threatened to consume me again, a wave crashing over my fragile sanity.

In that moment, I made a choice. I would write. I would pour my heart onto the page, channeling my fears, my hopes, and my love for him into words. I scrambled for my Artsy Diary, the one where I documented everything: my thoughts, my dreams, and the fragments of conversations we had shared.

The pages felt worn under my fingertips, each line a testament to my journey, both beautiful and painful. As I scribbled, the words flowed like a river, a cathartic release that washed away some of the heaviness.

"I can't lose you to the silence," I wrote, tears spilling onto the paper. "Even if we are apart, my love for you remains an indelible part of who I am."

I could feel the pressure in my chest start to ease, the act of writing liberating me in a way I had long forgotten. I wrote about the dreams we shared, the laughter that echoed beneath the tree, and the unbearable silence that now defined my nights.

As dawn broke, spilling soft light into my room, I felt a flicker of hope ignited within me. The panic subsided, replaced by the warmth of a new day and the promise of healing. I couldn't erase the past, but I could embrace it, wear it like a badge of honor—a testament to a love that had shaped me, even if it had left scars.

Maybe, just maybe, I could find a way to navigate this tangled web of love and loss. With the sun rising outside, I finally understood: I had a story to tell, and it was mine—beautiful, messy, and uniquely my own.

PART 7 - THE MESSAGE

"I love you, butterflies soar, In a garden where hearts explore. But 'I don't like you anymore,' Is the knife that shatters, leaves you sore."

Morning light filtered through my curtains, but instead of warmth, it felt cold and distant. I jolted awake, heart racing, the remnants of nightmares clinging to my mind like shadows refusing to let go. My dreams had twisted into something grotesque, filled with images of him disappearing, his laughter echoing in the void, haunting me as if warning me of an impending loss.

The need to clear the chaos swirling around me consumed my thoughts. I couldn't afford to dwell on the darkness—I needed to get to Theo's house first. Every minute I spent in this haze felt like a wasted moment, a betrayal of the urgency that surrounded us.

"Mom, I'm heading out to meet some friends!" I called, forcing a casual tone that betrayed the anxiety clawing at my insides.

"Be safe, Daisy!" she replied, but there was an edge of worry in her voice that made my heart sink further.

I caught her gaze lingering on me, a mother's intuition piercing through the facade I tried to maintain. I grabbed my bike and pedaled furiously toward Theo's house, the wind whipping against my face, a futile attempt to clear my head.

Each rotation of the pedals felt like a countdown, each gust of wind a reminder that time was slipping away. When I reached his door, I knocked urgently. He opened it almost immediately, his expression a mix of relief and worry, dark circles under his eyes revealing sleepless nights.

"Are you ready?" I asked, and he nodded, but something in his gaze made my stomach twist.

It was the look of someone grappling with their own demons, their own fears threatening to spill over. Together, we headed to the police station, where officers were coordinating a search effort. The tension was palpable; the air thick with unspoken fear.

I glanced around at the faces of the officers, some frowning over maps, others on phones, their voices low and urgent.

After a brief discussion, we learned a group was gathering at the waterfall, scouring the area for any signs of him.

A chill ran down my spine at the thought of everyone searching, desperate to find answers, but I sensed an undercurrent of something sinister—a trap waiting to ensnare us all.

"Let's go," Theo urged, determination flickering in his eyes, but his unease mirrored mine.

When we arrived at the waterfall, the serene beauty of the scene felt at odds with the growing dread that clung to me. The sound of cascading water, usually a source of calm, now felt like a cruel reminder of the turmoil beneath the surface.

Officers and volunteers were moving about, searching the banks and combing through the brush, their shouts echoing against the rocks.

I felt a nagging sensation that we were being watched, that unseen eyes were tracking our every move.The area was alive with chaos, but I couldn't shake the feeling of isolation.

My mind drifted to the whispers of the past few days—the murmurs of the town, the rumors, the faces that wore concern but held back secrets. With everyone preoccupied, I felt a pull toward the woods nearby, an instinct that urged me to discover what lay hidden beneath the surface.

As I stepped into the dense foliage, the air thickened, an unsettling silence enveloping me. Each step felt heavier, as if the ground beneath me was sinking into a void of uncertainty.

Then my gaze landed on a piece of paper stuck to a tree, fluttering slightly in the breeze. My heart began to race, a mixture of dread and curiosity swirling within me.

As I approached, the shadows deepened, and a chill seeped into my bones. I reached out to peel it from the bark, my breath catching in my throat, the forest seemingly holding its breath.

Written in jagged, dark ink were the words:

"I thought you were the one I could trust, But trust me now, it's all gone to dust. Beneath the roots where secrets hide, You'll find what's left of the love I tried. I watched as you wandered, thinking you're free, But I'm always near, just wait and see. The truth will come out; it won't be sweet, The blood on your hands will make you weep."

A cold sweat broke out on my skin, and I staggered back, the world around me fading into a blur. The message sent chills coursing through my veins, and I felt as if the forest had come alive, watching, waiting, its breath heavy with malevolence.

My heart raced as my thoughts spiraled, grasping for a sense of logic in the madness.What did this mean? Who had written it? I turned the paper over, hoping for a clue, but it was blank—just an empty void mirroring the dread pooling in my stomach. The trees seemed to lean closer, their gnarled branches reaching out like skeletal fingers.

The stillness around me felt oppressive, as if the very air conspired to silence my cries. I turned and ran back to the others, the paper crumpling in my hand, a tangible reminder of the darkness lurking just out of sight.

As I burst back into the clearing, my heart raced. I needed to warn Theo. I needed to find him before whatever was out there found us first—and before the one who should have been our ally turned out to be our greatest threat.

"Daisy!" Theo's voice called, pulling me from my racing thoughts. He was standing near a cluster of officers, their attention directed toward the water's edge.

"What did you find?"

His eyes bore into mine, an urgency laced with concern.

"I—" My voice faltered as I glanced down at the crumpled note in my hand. I hesitated, unsure if I should reveal its contents. The weight of the words threatened to crush me.

"I found something in the woods... a note."

"What did it say?" Theo pressed, moving closer, and I could see the fear creeping into his expression.

I opened my hand, revealing the note, and watched asTheo's face paled, his eyes darting across the sinister words. A shudder ran through him, and for a moment, he looked almost unrecognizable, a mixture of anger and fear flashing across his features.

"This isn't just a message," he muttered, looking around as if the trees themselves might have ears.

"This feels like a warning... or a threat."

"We need to show this to the police," I said, my voice trembling as I fought against the weight of fear pressing down on me.

"They need to know someone's out there, someone who knows us."

But as we turned to find an officer, the forest seemed to whisper around us, a cold breeze rustling the leaves as if it held secrets of its own. The search party moved like shadows in the distance, oblivious to the danger lurking just beneath the surface.

"Daisy, wait," Theo said, grabbing my arm.

"What if this is a trap? What if they want us to lead them to the police? We don't know who wrote this."

His words chilled me to the bone.

"What do you suggest then? Just sit back and hope for the best?" I snapped, frustration boiling over."

"No, I just think we need to be cautious. If this note is linked to him..."

His voice trailed off, and we exchanged a look filled with unspoken fears. As we stood there, the chaos of the waterfall faded into the background, and the world around us shrank to just the two of us, wrapped in a cocoon of uncertainty. Every second felt like an eternity as I contemplated the enormity of the situation. I took a deep breath, steeling myself.

"We need to keep looking, Theo. We need to figure this out before it's too late."

His expression softened, and I saw the flicker of resolve in his eyes.

"Alright. But we do this smart. No rushing in blindly."

We turned back toward the search party, adrenaline surging through my veins, ready to face whatever lay ahead. But a nagging feeling lingered at the back of my mind, a sense of impending danger that wrapped around me like a shroud.

Together, we moved forward, but the weight of the note was a constant reminder that trust was a fragile thing.

As we plunged deeper into the unknown, I couldn't shake the feeling that someone was watching us, waiting for the perfect moment to strike.

PART 8 - THE WEIGHT OF EVIDENCE

After leaving the police station, the ride home felt eerily quiet. My mind was racing with too many thoughts at once. The note from the woods, Theo's troubled expression, the search party—it was all spiraling out of control. But one thing kept tugging at me: the bracelet I found.

When I finally walked through the door, my mom was waiting in the kitchen, sipping her coffee.

"Hey, sweetie, that's a nice bracelet. Who gave you that?" she asked, her eyes narrowing slightly in curiosity.

For a second, my heart skipped. I glanced down at my wrist and saw it, almost forgetting I had slipped it on. "Oh... uh, one of my friends," I mumbled, avoiding her eyes. She raised an eyebrow but didn't press further. I wasn't ready to explain. Not yet.

I darted upstairs to my room, shut the door behind me, and stood there, staring at the bracelet.

The light caught the tiny, dark specks embedded in its marble-like pattern, and something about it felt... off. I walked to my mirror, unhooked the bracelet from my wrist, and hung it on the small mole at the mirror's edge, the one I always used for my necklaces.

"I found this in the woods," I muttered to myself, "and didn't tell Theo or the cops... but I'm going to figure out whose it is."

I paced around the room, my thoughts spinning. I needed answers, and there was only one person I could trust with this. I grabbed my phone and texted my best friend, Maya. "Can you come over? It's urgent."

Not ten minutes later, Maya arrived, worry already creasing her face as she stepped through my door.

"What's going on, Daisy? You sounded freaked out."

I wasted no time and blurted out everything—the note, the bracelet, the strange feeling gnawing at me. She listened, her eyes widening as the story unfolded. Finally, I pointed to the bracelet still hanging from the mirror.

"I didn't give this to the police because I need to know where it came from. I need to know whose it was. But... I can't do this alone. Can you help me check his profile?" I asked, my voice a little shaky.

Maya nodded and pulled out her phone, unlocking it swiftly. "You want me to pull up his account?"

I nodded, my heart pounding in my chest as she typed my ex-boyfriend's name into the search bar.

There it was, his Instagram profile. Everything about it seemed the same at first glance—except for one thing. His bio had changed.

"In a museum full of art..." I whispered, reading aloud. My stomach dropped. The words felt ominous, like they carried some hidden meaning.

Maya frowned, scrolling through his page. "That's new. And weird. Who puts that in their bio?"Something felt fishy, but it didn't stop there. As Maya scrolled through his followers, I caught sight of a girl's profile that made my skin crawl. Her bio read, "I only had my eyes on you."

"What the hell?" Maya muttered. "These bios... it's like they're speaking to each other."A sense of dread washed over me. I wasn't sure why, but something about this girl, and her connection to my ex, didn't feel right.

"Her account is private," Maya pointed out. "We can't see anything unless..."

"Do you think she's involved with him?" I asked, feeling the knot in my stomach tighten.

Maya's lips pressed into a thin line. "We could use my backup account to follow her, see what she's posting. But even if we do, I'm not sure what we'll find."

My gaze drifted back to the bracelet on the mirror. Something about the way it gleamed in the dim light... the strands of what looked like dried blood along its band.

"I saw this bracelet in one of his highlights," I whispered, a chill creeping down my spine. Maya stared at me. "Are you sure?"

I grabbed the bracelet and brought it closer, comparing it with a photo on his profile. There it was—in a highlight from weeks ago: a coffee cup, two hands holding, and one of them wearing the same bracelet.

"It's the same," I whispered, my throat tightening. "It's the exact same one."

For a moment, the room seemed to spin. I felt nauseous. What did this mean? I frantically searched Google for any trace of the bracelet, scrolling through small jewelry businesses until I found it—a local artisan who customized bracelets. My fingers trembled as I messaged the shop, asking how many had been made.

The reply came quickly.

"I usually make tons, but that one's special. It was customized with the customer and her girlfriend's blood. I don't make those anymore—just that one, and it was the last."

I stared at the message, my pulse thundering in my ears. "Maya... this bracelet was made with blood. Their blood."

Her eyes went wide. "Daisy, what... what do you think that means?"

I couldn't respond.

Maya placed a hand on my shoulder. "What's wrong?"

I swallowed hard, fighting back the tears.

"I think he has a new girlfriend," I whispered, my voice cracking.

Maya's expression softened, but there was an awkward pause before she spoke.

"I thought of telling you, but I didn't want to hurt you. He seems happy... really happy. I'm sorry, Daisy."

I forced a bitter smile and shook my head. "No, it's fine. Really."

Maya frowned. "Do you want me to stay? Should I come to your place tonight?"

I sighed. "No, it's okay. I'll be fine."

After she left, I sat there, staring at the bracelet. An hour passed in silence before my mom's voice cut through the quiet.

"Daisy! Look who is here to see you!"

I made my way downstairs, expecting Theo or maybe even an officer, but I froze when I saw Maya standing there again, holding a box of donuts.

"Surprise!" she said, grinning.

"What happened?" I asked, bewildered.

"I'm staying with you tonight," she declared, and before I could protest, she dragged me back upstairs.

As we reached my room and I closed the door, she caught sight of the jacket hanging on the chair.

"Wait, is that my brother's jacket?" she asked, stepping closer to examine it.

I blinked, staring at her in shock. "What do you mean, your brother's jacket?"

She fumbled for her phone, opening her gallery and showing me a photo. Sure enough, it was the same jacket. I tried to brush it off. "There are tons like this, Maya. It can't be his."

"You said it was at the bar, right? A day ago, my brother came home soaking wet, and my dad asked why he didn't have a raincoat. He said he had a jacket but gave it to a girl who felt cold."

I stared at her, the room closing in as my mind raced. "Maya... what's going on?"

PART 9 - THE ARRIVAL OF ERIC

Eric had been away for years, leaving for the States when he was just 18 to pursue his undergrad degree in economics. Now, at 23, he had recently finished his MBA. In the six years that had passed, the image I had of him—awkward, lanky, and always buried in textbooks—had completely transformed. If I had seen him that night at the bar, I "should" have recognized him instantly... but the truth is, I didn't.

Maybe it was because he had changed so much, or maybe it was because he barely looked at me, slipping away before I could make the connection. He wasn't the boy I remembered anymore. He had grown taller, his frame broader, and his demeanor more confident—miles away from the shy kid I used to know.

Maya, though, was my constant. She came from a family that seemed to have everything—businesses, money, and a life of luxury most people only dreamed of. Her parents owned resorts all across the States, but it was the one by the waterfall that always held a special place for both of us. It was an absolute dream, a perfect escape from reality.

We used to spend hours there, exploring the grounds, lounging by the pool, or having our little adventures. Sometimes, we'd just sit on the terrace overlooking the falls, talking about nothing and everything.

Maya had always been the friend who made me forget about the world's problems, even just for a while.

That night, after we shared our theories about the jacket and the strange connection to her brother, she offered a solution. "Let's talk to Eric tomorrow," she suggested, her voice steady and confident. "I'll text him. We'll meet at the resort." I nodded, grateful for her support.

She pulled out her phone and typed, "Be ready by 10 AM. Pick me up from Daisy's house, and we'll all go to the resort together." His response came almost immediately—"Okay," he replied within seconds.

After that, Maya did what she always knew would make me feel better. She pulled out a book and started reading aloud, her voice soft and calming. I loved it when people read to me, especially Maya. She had this way of making even the worst situations feel a little lighter, a little less overwhelming. As her voice wove the words together, the tension in my chest eased, and slowly, sleep took over.---

The next morning, I woke to the smell of breakfast drifting through the house. My mom had gone all out, cooking pancakes, eggs.. Maya and I sat at the table, the warmth of the food and the soft sunlight streaming through the windows helping to ground me in the moment.

For just a second, everything felt normal again—until the sound of an engine roaring outside pulled me from my thoughts.

I stepped outside and froze when I saw Eric's car—a sleek Aston Martin DB12 Volante, gleaming in a stunning Magneto Bronze. It looked like something straight out of a movie, the kind of car that made your heart race just looking at it. The sight of it made my breath hitch, but nothing compared to when I saw him step out.

Eric had changed. He wasn't the lanky, awkward teenager I remembered. He was tall now, muscular, his face sharp and defined. His dark hair was perfectly styled, and his clothes looked effortless like he'd just stepped off a magazine cover. For a moment, I couldn't speak. I was too stunned to even form words. The boy I once knew was gone, replaced by this... man.

If I hadn't recognized him that day at the bar, it made sense now. He was unrecognizable, his presence almost overwhelming. The way he moved, the confidence in his stride—it was impossible to reconcile with the memory I had of him.

"Morning," he said, his voice deeper than I remembered. It sent a shiver down my spine.

I managed to pull myself together, forcing a smile. "Morning. You... look different."

Eric chuckled, a small, knowing smile tugging at the corners of his mouth. "Time does that."

Maya nudged me, her grin wide as she looked between the two of us. "Told you he's changed."

I couldn't help but agree, still caught off guard by how good he looked. There was something about him now—something magnetic. It felt almost unsettling to think that he had been so close to me at the bar, offering me his jacket without a word, disappearing into the night like a ghost.

We drove in silence for a while, the sound of the engine humming softly against the backdrop of my thoughts. Eric occasionally stole glances at me, his expression a mixture of concern and curiosity. I found myself lost in the details of our surroundings—the vibrant green trees swaying gently in the breeze, the sunlight filtering through the leaves, casting playful shadows on the road. It was a stark contrast to the turmoil swirling in my mind.

As we arrived at the resort, the air was thick with the scent of blooming flowers and fresh mountain air. Maya had always described it as a dream, and standing there, I could finally see why. The cascading waterfall in the distance glistened under the afternoon sun, its soothing sound creating a serene atmosphere. But beneath that beauty, I felt a weight on my heart.

Maya stepped out first, her usual confident stride on full display. But before I could follow, Eric came around the car quickly, pulling open the door for me before I even reached for the handle.

For a moment, I just stared, caught off guard. It felt... surreal, almost like something out of a movie. My heart fluttered in a way I wasn't expecting.

My ex never did things like this for me. And suddenly, I realized, there's a difference between a boy and a man. But still, I couldn't let myself get carried away—one small gesture didn't mean anything. Or did it?

I ran my fingers through my hair, trying to keep my cool as I stepped out of the car. "Thanks," I murmured, feeling a little awkward under his gaze.

Maya, who had been watching the whole thing, shot Eric a look. "I've never seen this side of you before," she teased. "Well, I'm a girl too, y'know. I deserve that kind of treatment!"

Eric just shrugged with a faint smile. "What, should I have opened the door for you too?" His voice, low and smooth, sent a shiver down my spine—like his words were brushing against my skin. There was something about the way he spoke that made the simplest comment feel charged, like every syllable had weight.

Maya rolled her eyes, grinning. "Whatever. Did you bring the card? I don't have mine—it's probably somewhere at home."

"Yeah, it's in the glove box," he replied, nodding toward the car.

Maya walked over to grab it, but I stayed still for a moment, watching Eric out of the corner of my eye. There was something about him. The way he carried himself, the subtle confidence in his movements.

Every time he spoke, his voice had this gentle authority to it, like he didn't need to raise it to be heard. It resonated deep, in a way that made my chest feel tight.

Maya swiped the card to unlock the door, and we walked inside. But even as the day unfolded, I couldn't shake the feeling that something was different, that Eric was different. And I wasn't sure what to make of it.

PART 10 - THREADS OF SUSPENSION

As we walked through the front door of the resort, Eric stepped ahead and, with a slight bow, gestured toward me. "You first, madam," he said, his voice smooth and confident. I could feel a blush threatening to rise, but I quickly stifled it, offering him a small, awkward smile as I stepped inside.

Before I could even process the warmth of the place, I heard Maya's startled voice echoing from another room.

"Daisy!" she shouted her tone a mix of surprise and alarm.

I rushed toward her, finding her staring down at the floor, pointing at something with wide eyes. The paintings. The ones we'd made when we were 15. They were now lying on the ground, the glass frames shattered, and the open window nearby was likely the cause.

"My heart..." Maya said, her voice breaking a little as she knelt down, gingerly picking up one of the pieces. "The frame is broken," she whispered sadly.

I knelt beside her, feeling the same pang of sadness. Those drawings were a part of us, a piece of our shared history, and seeing them like this hurt. The carefree summer days when we spent hours painting at the resort now felt so far away.

Eric walked in, fashionably late as always. He looked down at us, his expression softening as he saw the mess.

"I can fix that, ladies," he said, stepping toward us. "By the way, how long has it been since you both were here?"

Maya and I exchanged a glance, her eyebrow raising in a silent conversation. "About a year," I said, and Maya nodded.

"Ah, so that's why you wanted to come back after so long," Eric said, as though putting the pieces together.

Maya and I looked at each other again, our silent conversation continuing. We both knew the real reason for being here wasn't just a simple visit to the resort. We needed to talk to Eric about that night at the bar.

Maya gave me an expectant look, silently telling me to ask him. But I was too nervous—what if he didn't remember? What if he did? I gave her a pleading look in return, shaking my head ever so slightly.

Eric caught on to our wordless exchange, smirking. "Ladies, may I ask what's going on between you two? Is this some secret code I'm not in on?"

Maya rolled her eyes, grabbed his hand, and led him into the living room, with me trailing behind. As we sat down, she didn't waste any time.

"So, Eric," she began, her tone casual but her eyes serious. "You said you gave your jacket to a girl that night at the bar, right?"

He blinked, his expression turning puzzled. "Which night?"

"The night at the bar, a few days ago," Maya clarified, her tone sharpening slightly.

"Oh, that," Eric said, leaning back and trying to recall. "Yeah, I remember. What about it?"

Maya's gaze narrowed as she leaned in. "Who was the girl?"

Eric looked genuinely confused for a second, rubbing the back of his neck. "I didn't really know her," he admitted. "She was sitting at the bar, shivering, and I could see water dripping from her dress. She looked miserable, so I gave her my jacket. Why?"

I froze, remembering how I had felt that night—the cold, the wet clothes, and the sudden warmth of the jacket.

Maya wasn't letting him off that easy. "So you just dropped your jacket on some random girl?"Eric shrugged. "Yeah, I saw her shivering. I couldn't just leave her there like that. It felt... wrong."

There was something about the way he said it—so sincere, so understanding. I could see how much he cared, even for a stranger. That side of him was new to me. I couldn't help but feel my heart soften a little.

Maya sighed. "Well, did she at least thank you?"

Maya crossed her arms, raising an eyebrow at Eric. "Well, did she at least thank you?"

Eric shook his head slightly, a thoughtful expression crossing his face. "I don't think she did," he said, pausing for a second. "Actually... I didn't really see her face. I rushed out of the bar right after giving her the jacket."

I blinked in surprise. "Wait, you didn't see her face?"

Eric leaned back, rubbing his chin. "Yeah, I had to take an important call. It was getting too noisy in there, so I headed out the back. I don't think she saw me either."

He glanced between us, his brow furrowing. "I didn't really think much of it. She looked cold, and I just acted without really expecting anything in return."

Maya and I exchanged another look. It was strange—Eric had given his jacket to a girl he didn't even see, and then just disappeared? Something didn't add up, but I couldn't tell if it was because of the situation itself or if it was my own nervousness clouding my judgment.

"So, you just left?" Maya asked, her voice slightly incredulous. "Didn't you think to check on her later?"

Eric shrugged. "No, not really. I assumed she'd be fine with the jacket. The call was urgent, and by the time I was done, I didn't see her again." He looked genuinely perplexed by our line of questioning.

Maya sat back, pursing her lips. "Weird."

Eric looked at her, confused. "Why are you so interested in this? Is something wrong?"

Maya glanced at me, giving me a subtle nod, silently asking if I wanted to push further. I hesitated, unsure of what to say next. Eric's explanation seemed genuine, and yet... something still felt off.

Part 11 - Intimate Confessions

After some time, Eric looked at his phone and said, "Don't go upstairs," before stepping outside to take a call. Maya turned to me, trying to lighten the mood. "It's nothing, Daisy, just a jacket. He probably didn't even think twice about it. Don't stress."

I exhaled, forcing a small smile. "Yeah, you're right. It's no big deal."

Maya nodded but then glanced toward the staircase. "Still, what do you think is upstairs? He specifically said not to go up. That's suspicious, don't you think?"

I shrugged, playing it off. "Probably nothing. Just some random stuff."

But Maya's curiosity wasn't so easily dismissed. "Let's go check it out."

I hesitated, but my feet followed hers up the stairs. When we reached the top, we were greeted by a door with a ridiculous sign: "Do Not Enter—Eric's Private Lair (Seriously, Stay Out!)" It was childish, the kind of thing you'd expect to see on a teenager's room.

Maya grinned, clearly amused. "Classic Eric," she muttered as her hand reached for the doorknob.

Just as she was about to twist it open, her phone rang. She glanced at the screen. "It's my mom. Hold on," she whispered. "Don't go in without me, I'll be back in a second."

She stepped away, leaving me alone in front of the door. I stared at the sign, curiosity pulling at me, but I stopped myself. I shouldn't. Eric's warning echoed in my head, but the temptation was strong.

Just then, I heard Eric's voice from downstairs. "Hey, where did you go?"

I jumped slightly, then hurried back toward the staircase. "I, uh, just went upstairs," I said casually, hoping he wouldn't notice anything suspicious.

Eric appeared at the bottom of the stairs, leaning against the railing, his eyes scanning me. "Upstairs, huh?" His tone was light, but there was something unreadable in his expression.

Before I could answer, Maya came back, still on her phone, but she caught my eye and immediately knew what was going on. She glanced at Eric, who seemed oblivious, and then back at me with a knowing look. She understood, and her expression was clear: Don't worry, I'll handle this.

"Actually," I cut in, trying to change the subject. "The view from the balcony is incredible. You should check it out."

Eric raised an eyebrow but nodded. "Yeah? I'll take a look in a bit."

Maya gave me a subtle nod of approval as I desperately tried to steer the conversation away from what just happened. It seemed to work, though I couldn't shake the feeling that Eric knew more than he was letting on.

As Eric moved near the balcony, Maya turned to me with an apologetic look. "My mom wants me home. Some of her friends were asking about her, and she booked a cab. Can you please drop Daisy off on your way back?"

I shot her a pleading expression, silently begging her not to leave me alone. But she shrugged, a mixture of regret and determination in her eyes. "I need to go, sorry."

"Fine," I muttered, feeling a wave of disappointment wash over me.

Eric smirked, his tone laced with sarcasm. "I won't kill you or leave you here alone, you know," he said, clearly trying to lighten the mood.

Once the cab arrived, Maya left, and I found myself standing awkwardly with Eric. He stepped closer to the balcony, his fingers deftly working to undo the buttons on his shirt. I tried to look away, but my eyes betrayed me, captivated by the sensuality of his movements. Each button released, revealing a glimpse of toned skin beneath.

As he faced the breathtaking view of the waterfall, he rubbed his hair with one hand, retrieving a cigarette from his pants pocket. I felt a rush of heat in my cheeks when he caught me staring.

"Um, that's a nice table," I stammered, gesturing awkwardly toward where he had dropped his shirt.

"What?" he smirked, stepping closer, his expression teasing as he took my hand and led me near the table. "This table?"

His scent enveloped me—strong and divine, like a mix of cedar and something uniquely him. "Uh, yeah, the marble looks pretty," I managed, trying to sound casual.

"Well, my dad got this from England," he replied, locking his gaze onto mine, sending shivers down my spine.

At that moment, the world around us faded, and all I could think of was the electricity sparking between us. As I couldn't meet his gaze any longer, a rush of anxiety surged through me, and I sank onto the couch near the table, my heart racing.

Eric slightly bent down, and the smoky tendrils of his cigarette curled around my ears, sending shivers down my spine. The way he carried himself was almost magnetic, like a hot villain who knew exactly the effect he had on others.

"Feeling overwhelmed?" he teased, a playful smirk dancing on his lips as he leaned closer. The warmth radiating from his body mixed with the intoxicating scent of his cologne made it hard to focus.

I nodded, trying to play it cool, but my cheeks were probably flushed. "Just... taking it all in," I managed to say, hoping my voice didn't betray the fluttering in my chest.

He chuckled softly, that deep, rich sound sending tingles through me. "You can relax, Daisy. I promise I'm not that scary," he said, the way he spoke almost intimate as if we were sharing a secret.

I glanced up at him, taking in the way the light caught his features—strong jawline, tousled hair, and those eyes that seemed to hold a world of mischief and intrigue. Just then, a breeze fluttered through the balcony, sending the faint scent of the nearby waterfall mingling with his cologne. It was a surreal moment, suspended between reality and something more.

"Really?" I replied, half-jokingly. "You look like you could take on an army."

He laughed again, the sound low and inviting. "Maybe I could, but for now, I'd rather just take you on a tour of this place. What do you say?"

I bit my lip, torn between wanting to run away and wanting to stay lost in this moment with him. The couch felt like a safe haven, but he was a magnet pulling me closer, promising an adventure I couldn't resist.

"Okay," I said, my heart pounding in my chest. "Lead the way."

PART 12 - BENEATH THE WATERFALL: A TANGLE OF TRUTHS

As we walked out onto the balcony, the stunning view of the waterfall momentarily took my breath away. But then my gaze fell on his watch—elegant and timeless, a stark contrast to the chaos swirling in my mind. It was as if the world around me faded, leaving just him and the thoughts racing through my head.

Eric reached for my hand, his grip warm and reassuring. As he led me away from the edge, the memory of the picture from Maya's phone resurfaced—the moment I had seen him and his girlfriend holding hands, the very bracelet I found glimmering on her wrist. A knot tightened in my stomach, and I fought to shake off the unease.

We walked along the path lined with blooming flowers, I couldn't help but steal glances at him. The way he moved with confidence, and the casual elegance he carried; it was captivating. Yet beneath that allure, there was a kindness that made me feel safe—a rare combination I hadn't expected.

As we wandered further, I spotted a secluded area near the waterfall. The sound of rushing water was soothing, and the setting felt almost magical. "What do you think?" I asked, gesturing to the spot.

"It's perfect," Eric said, a glint of excitement in his eyes. "Let's set up camp here."

We found a flat rock near the water's edge, and I sat down, watching the water cascade over the rocks, its rhythm calming my racing thoughts. Eric stood nearby, his silhouette framed by the sunlight filtering through the trees.

"Sometimes it's nice to just sit and listen," he said, his voice low as he joined me. "To let the world wash over you."

"Yeah, it is," I replied, feeling the tension in my shoulders start to ease.

We sat in comfortable silence for a while, the beauty of the surroundings wrapping around us. I found myself reflecting on everything that had happened—the bracelet, my ex, the uncertainty of it all. It felt good to share this moment with Eric, to have someone beside me who didn't expect me to be strong all the time.

"Daisy," he said softly, breaking the spell. "Are you alright?"

His voice was smooth, almost like velvet, and I found myself nodding, though the turmoil inside me lingered. I tried to focus on the present, to push away the doubts and fears, but the connection between us felt electric. Would I dare to explore this budding attraction when the shadow of his past loomed over us?

As we stepped further into the house, I glanced back at the waterfall. It was beautiful, yes, but it couldn't compete with the whirlwind of emotions surging within me. I took a deep breath, determined to embrace the moment, even if it meant risking heartbreak.

We moved deeper into the house, the sound of the waterfall fading as we entered a cozy sitting area. Eric glanced over at me, his brow furrowing slightly as he studied my expression. There was a moment of silence, filled with the distant rush of water and the soft rustle of leaves outside.

"Daisy," he said, his voice dropping to a softer tone. "I can see the fear in your eyes. What's going on? You look... frightened."

I flinched slightly, not expecting him to notice. But how could I hide the truth? The tears I had shed over the past few days had left their mark, making my eyes puffy and red, like a storm that had raged and now lingered in the aftermath.

"I've just... been through a lot," I managed to whisper, my throat tightening.

He stepped closer, his gaze searching mine. "You don't have to pretend around me, you know. I can tell you've been crying."

My heart raced. Could he really see the turmoil I tried to mask? I could feel his concern wrapping around me, a comforting but unsettling reminder of how vulnerable I felt.

In that moment, I was overwhelmed with emotion, and without thinking, I let the words spill out, a poetic line reflecting my state:

"With eyes like windows, sorrow's tide displayed, A fragile canvas where shadows have played."

Eric's expression softened, and he gently brushed his thumb along my cheek, as if to wipe away the remnants of my tears. I was caught between the warmth of his touch and the weight of my fears.

"Daisy, whatever it is, you don't have to face it alone," he said, his voice low and steady.

The sincerity in his words enveloped me, igniting a flicker of hope amid the storm brewing within.

I wanted to believe him, to let down my guard and share the weight I carried. But the fear of the unknown still lingered, threading through the air like a silent specter. Would opening up to him bring solace or further complicate the tangled web of emotions we were navigating together?

I took a deep breath, feeling the weight of my words pressing against my chest.

"Eric, I need to tell you what's been going on," I said, my voice trembling slightly.

"My ex, Tristan... he went missing. And while everyone keeps telling me not to worry, I can't shake this sadness I feel about it."

"What's your Ex-boyfriend's name?" Eric asked, his curiosity genuine.

I hesitated for a moment, the name feeling heavy on my tongue. "Tristan," I finally replied, my heart sinking as I spoke it aloud.

Eric's brow furrowed, a flicker of something unreadable crossing his features. "Tristan," he echoed softly, as if trying to place the name in his memory. "Is he the one who went missing?"

I nodded, swallowing hard. "Yeah, we broke up a while ago, but... I still care about him. I can't help but worry about what happened. I can't shake this feeling that something is wrong."

Eric took a step closer, the warmth of his presence enveloping me. "Daisy, it's okay to feel that way. You've been through so much," he said, his voice steady and reassuring. "But you're not alone in this. I promise to help you find the answers you need."

I looked into his eyes, feeling the sincerity of his words wash over me like a wave of relief. "Thank you, Eric," I said softly, feeling a flicker of hope ignite within me. "It means a lot to have your support."

He nodded, and for a moment, we stood there, the weight of our unspoken understanding hanging in the air. "Let's get moving," he said finally, breaking the tension. "We have a long road ahead, but we'll face it together."

With that, we stepped out into the fading sunlight, ready to face whatever lay ahead.

PART 13 - SAFE HAVENS

As we stepped inside, the air was tinged with the coolness of dusk, I glanced at Eric, his profile illuminated by the fading light, and felt a rush of gratitude for his presence.

"Where do we start?" I asked, breaking the silence that had settled between us.

"First, let's gather some information about Tristan," Eric suggested, his tone shifting to a more serious note. "Do you have anyone you can reach out to—friends or family who might know something?"

I nodded slowly, recalling the tight-knit circle of friends we used to share. "I can try reaching out to Mia, his sister. She's probably worried sick."

"Good idea," Eric said, his expression earnest. "Let's head back inside. You can use my phone if you need to."

As we walked back, I felt a surge of determination mixed with apprehension. The closer we got to the house, the more real the situation felt. Eric held the door open for me, and I stepped inside, taking a deep breath to steady myself.

"Let's find a quiet spot," I suggested, leading the way to a cozy nook by the fireplace. The warmth from the crackling flames offered some comfort, but the heaviness in my chest remained.

I took a seat on one of the plush couches, pulling out Eric's phone while he hovered nearby, his presence a steady anchor. My fingers trembled slightly as I dialed Mia's number, the sound of the ringing filling the space between us.

"Come on, pick up," I whispered to myself, willing her to answer. Just as doubt began to creep in, the line clicked, and Mia's voice came through, laced with concern.

"Daisy? Is that you?" she asked, relief washing over her tone.

"Mia, hey! I'm so sorry to bother you," I started, my heart racing. "I just wanted to check in. Have you heard anything about Tristan?"

There was a pause on the other end, and I could practically hear her thoughts racing. "No, I haven't," she replied, her voice shaky. "It's like he just vanished. I don't understand why no one has seen him."

"I feel the same way. I'm worried sick," I admitted, my throat tightening.

"But I need to know what happened. Is there anyone who might have seen him last?

"Maybe... I can ask around," Mia said slowly. "But I just don't know if that'll help. He was acting strange the last time I saw him."

"What do you mean?" I pressed, my curiosity piqued.

"Just... distant, you know? Like he was hiding something," she replied, and I felt a chill run down my spine.

"I'll let you know if I find out anything, okay?"

After saying goodbye, I hung up and looked at Eric, who had been quietly listening.

"What did she say?" he asked, concern etched on his face.

"Mia hasn't heard anything either. But she mentioned Tristan was acting strange before he went missing," I explained, trying to keep my voice steady despite the knot in my stomach.

Eric nodded, processing the information. "We need to dig deeper. There might be something at the bar—maybe someone remembers seeing him."

I felt a flicker of hope. "You really think so?"

"Absolutely. If he was there the night he disappeared, it's worth checking," Eric said, his confidence infectious.

"Alright, let's do it," I replied, determination settling in.

I glanced at Eric, who met my gaze with an encouraging smile.

"It's getting late. We should head back," I said, feeling a twinge of anxiety about the night ahead.

As we settled into the car, I took a deep breath, trying to shake off the unease.

"Let's talk more tomorrow. I don't want to get too tense about all this right now," Eric said, his voice steady as he started the engine.

"Yeah, that sounds good," I replied, grateful for his calmness.

The hum of the engine and the soft glow of the dashboard lights provided a sense of comfort as we drove through the quiet streets.

When we arrived at my house, Eric parked the car and turned to me, his expression softening.

"Hey, it's going to be okay," he said, his voice gentle.

Before I could respond, he leaned in and spontaneously kissed my forehead. I froze, surprise washing over me as a rush of warmth filled my chest. "Don't worry too much," he added, pulling back to meet my wide eyes.

For a moment, I felt a wave of safety wash over me, as if the weight of my worries had lightened just a bit. With Maya and Eric by my side, and the thought of Theo lingering in the back of my mind, I felt a flicker of hope.

"Thank you, Eric," I finally managed to say, my voice barely above a whisper as I stepped out of the car, still processing the unexpected intimacy of the moment.

"See you tomorrow," he replied, a reassuring smile on his lips before I closed the door.

As I stepped inside, the familiar warmth of home enveloped me, but the heaviness of the day still lingered.

My dad was in the living room, his newspaper spread out on the coffee table. He looked up, his brow lifting in a welcoming smile.

"How was your day, Daisy?" he asked, genuinely interested.

"Good!" I replied, forcing a smile that I hoped masked the whirlpool of emotions churning inside me.

"Just hung out with some friends."

"Anything exciting?" he pressed, his eyes twinkling with curiosity.

"Not really. Just... you know, the usual." I shrugged, trying to keep the details vague. The last thing I wanted was to dive into the chaos of my day.

"Glad to hear you're keeping busy," he said, returning to his newspaper. I loved how he tried to stay involved in my life, even when I didn't give him much to work with.

After exchanging a few more pleasantries, I made my way upstairs, feeling the weight of the world pressing down on my shoulders again.

Once inside my room, I plopped onto my bed, taking a moment to breathe deeply and center myself. The calm was short-lived, though, as my phone buzzed beside me.

I picked it up to find a message from Eric, and my heart raced at the sight of his name. "Hey, come to your window!" it read.

Intrigued, I quickly made my way to the window and peered outside. Sure enough, there was Eric, standing a few yards away with a playful grin on his face. He waved enthusiastically, his dark hair slightly tousled by the evening breeze.

I couldn't help but smile back, feeling a warmth spread through me. He looked so carefree at that moment, and it was contagious. I waved in response, my heart fluttering with a mix of excitement and disbelief.

"Goodnight!" he mouthed.

"Goodnight, Eric!" I called out softly, knowing he could hear me even from a distance. As he turned to leave, the warmth of our brief exchange lingered in the air, a little spark of happiness in a day filled with uncertainty.

I leaned against the window frame, feeling lighter than I had in a while, grateful for the unexpected moments that made everything feel a little bit easier.

PART 14 - THE MISSING LINK

The next day, the café buzzed with energy as the four of us gathered around a small table, the aroma of freshly brewed coffee wrapping around us like a warm embrace.

I glanced at Eric, Theo, and Maya, feeling a strange mix of comfort and tension in the air.

"So, what do you think happened to Tristan?" Maya asked, stirring her coffee absentmindedly.

Theo leaned back in his chair, his brows furrowed in thought. "It's hard to say. Do you think the note has anything to do with it?" he posed, his voice serious.

"That's what I'm wondering," I replied, my stomach tightening.

"Where did it come from? Did someone stick it there, or was it always there? It looked like ink, but it seemed too light. Almost like it was meant for someone else."

Eric nodded, his expression contemplative. "Or maybe it's a threat. What if someone's trying to intimidate him?"

The idea sent a shiver down my spine, and I exchanged worried glances with Theo.

"It's unsettling," Theo admitted. "But we can't jump to con-clusions. We need to consider all possibilities."

As the conversation continued, I felt a swell of anxiety rise within me. "And there's something else," I said, my voice drop-ping slightly as I tried to gather the courage to share.

"I found his girlfriend's bracelet in the woods."

Theo perked up, his attention shifting to me. "Bracelet? What are you talking about?"

I exchanged a glance with Maya and Eric, deciding to confide in them while keeping Theo in the dark for now.

"I saw it there, near the waterfall. I didn't tell you because I wanted to check it out on my own, but I'm sorry for not mentioning it before."

"What kind of bracelet?" Eric asked, leaning forward, his interest piqued.

"It was a delicate marble bracelet, stained with both Tristan's and his girlfriend's blood."

It seemed out of place, like it didn't belong there, I explained, feeling a knot of anxiety twist in my stomach.

"Did you show it to Mia?" Maya asked, her brow furrowing with concern.

"I didn't want to upset her further, especially if it has some-thing to do with Tristan," I admitted, glancing away, feeling guilty for keeping this from her.

"That makes sense," Eric said, his voice reassuring. "But we need to figure out if it's connected to what's going on."

Theo looked from me to Maya and Eric, his expression becom-ing serious. "This is starting to sound more dangerous than we thought. If someone's involved with Tristan's disappearance, we need to be careful."

"We will," I promised, determination hardening in my voice. "We just need to keep our eyes open and gather as much information as we can."

As we sat in the café, surrounded by the clinking of cups and soft chatter, the weight of our conversation hung heavy in the air.

We were diving deeper into a mystery that was proving to be far more complex than any of us had anticipated, but I felt a flicker of hope knowing I wasn't alone in this. With Maya, Theo, and Eric by my side, we would face whatever came next, together.

Eric leaned back in his chair, his expression thoughtful. "Let's meet Tristan's girlfriend. If Mia said he seemed off before he went missing, she might know something," he suggested, glancing around the table for support.

Theo nodded in agreement. "That sounds like a good idea."

Maya chimed in, her brow furrowed in thought. "But how can we meet her? We don't even know where she lives."

"It's easy," Eric replied confidently. "Just give me her name. Theo and I can go to her house; we have friends all over this city."

"I want to come too," Maya insisted, her determination shining through.

Eric shook his head, a teasing smile playing on his lips. "No, it's better if Theo and I handle this."

I watched the exchange, sensing the tension rising. "Why can't we all go?" I asked, curious about his reasoning.

After a moment of hesitation, Eric relented. "Alright, you can come. But let us take the lead, okay?"

With a nod, he pulled out his phone. "Let me see if I can get her address." He tapped away, his focus unwavering.

Within minutes, he looked up, a satisfied grin on his face. "Got it. Her name is Sarah, and she lives just a few blocks from here."

"Alright, what's the plan?" I asked, my heart racing at the thought of finally getting some answers.

"We'll meet up at Sarah's place after school tomorrow," Eric said, his eyes glinting with determination. "Theo and I will do the talking. You two can help keep things casual."

"Sounds good," Maya replied, her excitement bubbling over.

As we finalized our plans, I felt a mix of apprehension and hope. With Eric, Theo, and Maya by my side, maybe we could uncover the truth behind Tristan's disappearance and the mystery surrounding the bracelet I found.

As we arrived at Sarah's house, a hushed anticipation hung in the air.

Eric approached the door with a confidence that seemed to command attention, and we all followed his lead. He knocked, and the sound echoed like a heartbeat.

A few moments later, the door creaked open, revealing a disheveled man in his fifties. He squinted at us through the dim light. "What do you want?"

"Is Sarah here?" Eric asked, his voice steady despite the tension that was brewing around us.

The man shook his head. "She left about a week ago. Didn't say where she was going."

"Do you have any idea where she might have gone?" Theo pressed, his brow furrowed with concern.

"Nope, she's just a renter here," the man replied, his tone indifferent.

I felt a chill run down my spine. Sarah was missing, just like Tristan. Had the bracelet I found in the woods been a clue? Was she connected to his disappearance in some way? My heart raced with a mix of fear and curiosity.

"Can we look around?" Maya asked, her voice barely above a whisper.

The man shrugged, stepping aside. "Whatever. Just don't make a mess."

As we stepped into the dim hallway, the air felt heavy with secrets.

Eric led the way, his confidence unwavering, while Theo and Maya followed closely behind. I trailed behind, my thoughts swirling like a storm.

Each room we entered seemed to hold its own mysteries.

The furniture was sparse, almost as if Sarah had packed her life away in a hurry. I caught a glimpse of her bedroom door, slightly ajar. Something compelled me to move closer.

"Wait," Eric said suddenly, his sharp gaze scanning the space. "Something feels off."

My heart raced as I glanced back at him. "What do you mean?"

"I don't know. It's like... she left in a rush," he replied, his voice low and serious.

Eric's jaw tightened. "We need to figure out what happened here."

The realization hit me hard: Sarah wasn't just a missing person. She was part of a puzzle, a link to the darkness surrounding Tristan's disappearance.

A villain hiding in plain sight.

As we stood there, surrounded by uncertainty and fear, I felt a shift in the atmosphere. The thrill of the chase pulsed in my veins, urging us forward into the unknown.

Part 15 - Fractured Trust

As we walked out of the house, a heavy silence hung between us, the weight of unanswered questions pressing on all our minds. I glanced back at the door, still slightly ajar, the dim hallway behind it now feeling like a tunnel leading deeper into the unknown. Why had Sarah left so suddenly?

Theo was the first to break the silence. "Maybe she left because of Tristan," he said, his tone thoughtful, yet uneasy.

Eric shook his head, his jaw tight. "Tristan's missing, not dead—at least not yet. We don't know what's going on, but running off doesn't seem like something she'd do if she was just worried about him."

Maya frowned, her voice laced with doubt. "Exactly. If she really cared, wouldn't she be searching for him instead of disappearing herself? Leaving now... it doesn't make sense."

I nodded, the knot in my stomach tightening. "Especially since we found her bracelet at the falls. Why would it be there?"

Theo's expression darkened as he considered this. "We should hand it over to the police. If they see it was found near where Tristan disappeared, they'll have to investigate further."

I hesitated, my heart racing. "But what if they don't take it seriously? What if they just brush it off and decide it's another case of someone falling into the waterfall? They could close it quickly, show us some random body, and call it an accident or a mistake."

Eric glanced at me, his eyes narrowing slightly. "You really think they'd do that?"

"I don't know," I admitted, the words catching in my throat. "But my heart says something's wrong with Sarah. I can feel it."

We all exchanged a glance, the unease between us growing thicker with each passing second. The mystery was getting deeper, and nothing was adding up. Sarah leaving, Tristan's disappearance, the cryptic note at the falls—it all felt connected somehow, but we were still missing too many pieces.

Maya wrapped her arms around herself, as if trying to ward off a chill. "So, what now?"Theo glanced at Eric, then back to me. "We keep digging. If something's wrong with Sarah, we need to find out what—and fast."

Eric nodded, his eyes steady on mine. "We're not stopping until we figure this out. Sarah's hiding something, and it's only a matter of time before we uncover it."

We all decided to head to the woods near the waterfall, the place where I'd found the bracelet. The air was thick with tension and uncertainty, but something about moving forward felt necessary, like we were being pulled by invisible strings. The deeper we got into the forest, the more uneasy Theo looked.

"Are you sure about this?" Theo asked, his voice barely above a whisper. "This place gives me the creeps."

Eric, always quick with a snarky comeback, smirked. "What's the matter, Theo? Scared of some trees? Don't worry, I'll protect you. Maybe you can hold my hand if it gets too spooky."

Theo shot him a glare, but Eric just laughed, arrogance dripping from his voice. I couldn't help but smile at the banter—it was Eric's way of lightening the mood, even if he was a little too cocky sometimes.

As we ventured further, the trees thickened, their branches seeming to close in around us. The shadows stretched long under the setting sun, making the woods feel like a maze. We walked for hours, our eyes scanning the ground for any clues, but nothing stood out—no signs, no trails, nothing but the quiet rustle of leaves underfoot.

"This isn't right," Maya suddenly said, her voice cutting through the stillness. "I don't like this. We've gone too far."

Theo nodded, his usual confidence shaken. "She's right. Something feels off."

I could feel the tension creeping up on us, but I didn't want to stop. Not yet. "We can't just turn back now. We're close to figuring something out, I can feel it."

Eric glanced at me, determination flickering in his eyes. "Exactly. We've come this far; let's push a little more. There's gotta be something out here—we just haven't found it yet."

Theo groaned, clearly uneasy, rubbing the back of his neck. "Yeah, we've been saying that for, what? Four hours now? And all we've found is a whole lot of nothing. Plus, my stomach feels weird. Light, like I haven't eaten in forever."

Eric smirked at Theo's complaint, shaking his head. "What are you, a toddler? We'll grab food after. But we're not leaving until we find something."

Theo sighed, his reluctance clear, but Eric's words carried an unshakable confidence that somehow pulled us forward again.

We kept moving, reaching a steep incline where the soft sand made climbing tricky. I hesitated for a second, trying to find stable footing when suddenly, my foot slipped out from under me.

Before I could even gasp, Eric's hand shot out, grabbing me by the waist, pulling me close—so close that for a split second, our faces were inches apart, and I could feel his breath on my skin.

Time seemed to stop. My heart raced as I realized just how close we were, his hands steadying me, his lips nearly brushing mine. There was no space between us, not even enough for air to pass. It was both terrifying and thrilling at the same time, a moment that felt too perfect to be real.

"Careful," Eric whispered, his voice low and soft, sending shivers down my spine.

I swallowed hard, my cheeks flushing as I managed to nod. "Thanks."

His grip loosened, but the moment lingered, an electric charge hanging between us. As we continued walking, I couldn't shake the feeling that something had shifted—something more than just our investigation.

Eric. The way he held me, the way he was always there, steady and strong. I didn't want to admit it to myself, but I could feel my heart tugging in his direction. But at the same time, guilt gnawed at me. Tristan. I couldn't ignore that I'd once cared for him deeply, and now here I was, falling for someone else.

Later, when Theo and Eric moved ahead, I found myself walking next to Maya. The thoughts that had been swirling in my mind since Eric grabbed me spilled out.

"Maya, I... I can't help but notice how Eric always seems to be there for me," I said, my voice barely above a whisper. "It feels different, you know? Like there's something more between us."

Maya's eyes lit up with excitement, a grin spreading across her face. "Oh my god! You're crushing on my brother?" She sounded more thrilled than I expected.

I bit my lip, nodding. "Yeah... but it feels complicated. Tristan's missing, and I'm just confused."

Maya shook her head, brushing it off with a smile. "Daisy, it's not complicated at all. Tristan's your ex, not your lover. You're not cheating on him or anything. He's the one who moved on first, remember? He got into a relationship with Sarah, not you."

I swallowed, the guilt still lingering. "But when we broke up, Tristan said he wasn't going to be in another relationship for a while. And then there was Sarah..."

Maya's expression softened as she placed a hand on my arm. "Listen, Tristan might have said that, but people change, Daisy. He made his choices, and you're allowed to make yours. My brother, Eric, he's good for you. He's different now, not the cranky, lame guy he used to be."

I glanced at her, surprised by her support. "You think I deserve him?"

"I think you both deserve each other," she said, smiling warmly. "Don't think about Tristan like that. We're searching for him because he's a good friend, and we're worried. But this—what's happening between you and Eric—is something real. Don't let the past hold you back."

Her words hung in the air, and for the first time in a long while, I felt a sense of clarity. Maya was right. My feelings for Tristan were in the past. But with Eric, something new and unexpected was blooming.

As we walked deeper into the woods, I couldn't help but steal a glance at Eric. My heart raced, but this time, it wasn't with confusion or fear. It was with the thrill of something new, something unknown.

I wasn't sure where this would lead, but I was ready to find out.

Part 16 - Unheard Cries

Just as we were beginning to regain our composure, a sudden thud echoed through the woods, causing Maya and me to jump. We turned to see Theo stumble and disappear below the rocky edge of a hidden hole, a gasp escaping my lips as I rushed toward the sound.

"Theo!" Eric screamed, his voice cracking with panic. The urgency in his tone pulled me into action as Maya and I sprinted after him.

"Can you hear me, Theo?" Eric shouted, his voice ringing out against the quiet of the woods. "Answer us!"

After what felt like an eternity, Theo's voice finally came back, faint but clear. "Yes! I can hear you! Just... it's dark down here!"

"Are you okay?" I called, my heart pounding in my chest.

"Everything's dark here. I feel frightened." His words sent chills down my spine, an icy grip of dread settling in.

Maya looked at me, her eyes wide with fear. "What do we do? We can't leave him!"

I glanced around, the weight of our predicament settling heavily on my shoulders. "We have to think," I said, trying to sound calm. "There's got to be a way to help him."

Maya's face fell, tears brimming in her eyes. "It's over. We're trapped," she whispered, her voice breaking.

"No, we're not trapped!" Eric said, his voice steady as he placed a reassuring hand on her shoulder. "Look! There's a path leading down alongside the canal. If we go down, we can reach him."

I nodded, steeling my resolve. "We'll walk unitedly. Theo can guide us from below."

Maya hesitated, glancing nervously at the dark abyss. "What if we get lost? What if we can't find our way back?"

"We can't go back now!" I insisted, my heart racing with the urgency of our situation. "We need to get to him."

Reluctantly, Maya nodded, and together we turned to face the dark path ahead. The uncertainty was palpable, our faces flushed with fear and adrenaline. Each step we took felt heavy, as if the ground itself was resisting our movement. The maze of rocky paths loomed around us, and Maya held her head in despair. "We're lost! We'll end up missing too!" she cried, the thought making my stomach twist in knots.

Theo's voice broke through again, cutting through the tension like a knife. "I can't keep my phone on much longer! We have to hurry!"

I glanced at Eric, who looked equally concerned. "We'll find a way out," he reassured me, but I could see the worry etched on his face.

With hearts pounding and fear clawing at us, we pressed on, each step echoing in the suffocating silence that enveloped us. The shadows grew longer, stretching out like grasping fingers as we descended deeper into the unknown.

Time felt distorted; every second dragged on endlessly, and with each passing moment, the absence of Theo's voice weighed heavier on our chests, our ears straining desperately for any sound, any hint of him.

"What do you think could have happened to him?" Maya's voice quivered, tinged with panic, as she cast a glance back toward the suffocating darkness we had come from.

Her wide eyes reflected the flickering light from our phones, filled with dread and uncertainty.

Suddenly, the silence felt thicker, and we all froze, our breath hitching in our throats. "Theo?" Eric called out, but the echo of his voice hung in the air, swallowed by the oppressive darkness. The absence of any reply sent a chill racing down my spine.

"There!" Eric's voice sliced through the tension as he pointed, urgency igniting in his eyes. A faint outline of a cave loomed ahead, its entrance gaping like a dark mouth, ready to swallow us whole. "Maybe he's in there!"

Holding onto each other, we approached the cave, fear and hope warring within us. I could see sorrow and determination in Eric's face as he gripped my hand tightly. He hadn't let go since we'd started this descent, his presence a comforting anchor in the swirling uncertainty.

Maya stood frozen for a moment, paralyzed by terror. Eric stepped in closer, wrapping his arms around her in a protective embrace. "It's okay, we'll get through this," he murmured, his voice steadying her.

Then he turned to me, his hands cupping my face gently. "It's okay, Daisy. We came this far together. I bet we'll find a way out—all of us." His sincerity ignited a flicker of hope within me.With our hearts racing, we stepped into the cave together.

The air grew cooler as we moved deeper, and the dampness clung to our skin. "Theo!" I called out, my voice echoing against the cavern walls, but silence followed my plea.

"Do you think he's okay?" Maya whispered, her voice shaking.

"He has to be," Eric replied, his determination palpable. "He's strong. We just need to find him."As we ventured deeper, the narrow passage opened up into a wider chamber, the shadows dancing around us.

The flickering light from our phones barely illuminated the cavern, casting eerie shapes on the walls. I felt an unsettling foreboding wash over me. "Where do you think this leads?" I wondered aloud, scanning the dark expanse.

"Maybe there's another way out," Eric suggested, moving ahead to inspect the walls, his footsteps steady against the stone. His determination was infectious, igniting a spark of hope in my chest.

Just then, a faint sound reached our ears—a soft echo that sent shivers down my spine. "Theo?" I called again, my heart racing at the possibility.

"I'm here!" Theo's voice floated back, relief flooding my veins. "Just follow the sound of my voice!"

We moved toward the sound, our hearts pounding in unison. The passage narrowed, and I could feel the rough walls pressing in on us. Eric glanced back at me, his expression a mix of concern and determination. He squeezed my hand tighter, grounding me as we pressed onward.

As we finally emerged into a larger cavern, there stood Theo, at the edge of a ledge overlooking a dark abyss. "You made it!" he exclaimed, relief washing over his face, and I felt a rush of warmth at the sight of him.

"Are you okay?" Maya rushed to his side, her voice filled with concern.

"I think so, but we need to get out of here," Theo said, looking at us with a mix of gratitude and fear.

"Okay, but first, let's find a way back up," Eric said, stepping forward to inspect our surroundings. "There has to be another exit somewhere."

As we regrouped, I noticed the bond between us strengthening in the face of danger.

Eric, Theo, and Maya were more than just friends—they were my lifeline, and I realized how much I valued each of them. But in that moment, I also felt something shift between Eric and me. The tension hung thick in the air, and every brush of our hands sent a jolt of electricity through me.

"Daisy," Eric said softly, breaking the silence. "We're going to get through this, I promise. I won't let anything happen to you or Maya."

His words wrapped around me like a warm blanket, and I couldn't help but feel a flutter in my chest. We had each other's backs, and in this dark cave, that felt like enough. "Let's stick together," I said, determination rising within me. "We'll find a way out—together."As we took a collective breath, I glanced at Eric, his unwavering gaze giving me strength. Whatever lay ahead, we would face it as one.

PART 17 - THE RING OF DESPAIR

The cold, damp air of the cave was heavy as we walked deeper into the shadows, our footsteps echoing against the stone walls. The farther we went, the more the scent of something foul began to creep in—sharp and pungent, like decaying flesh. It hit us all at once, and I instinctively covered my nose.

"What is that?" Eric muttered, his face twisted in disgust. Maya coughed, pulling her shirt up over her mouth.

I stepped forward, and suddenly, something soft squished beneath my foot. I froze. "Maya, shine your light over here."

She did, the beam trembling as it flickered over the ground. At first, we couldn't make sense of what we were looking at. It was a pale, fleshy color, mixed with white and brown, twisted and unrecognizable. My stomach lurched, but curiosity forced my hand. I crouched down, reaching for it, the texture wet and cold.

Then, in the dim light, I saw it—a human eye.

It stared back at me, still clinging to its eyelashes, wet and glossy. For a moment, time seemed to stop. My breath hitched, my heart pounding in my chest like it was going to explode.

"Oh my God, Maya!" I screamed, my voice breaking. The eye rolled in my palm as I staggered back. Maya's scream joined mine, echoing off the cave walls as I threw the eye down, my hand shaking uncontrollably. I felt bile rise in my throat, and my entire body trembled in horror.

Eric's eyes widened in disbelief as he caught sight of the eye now lying on the cave floor. "Daisy, what the hell—" he muttered, his voice low but thick with urgency. He bent down, grabbing my shoulders to steady me, his grip firm but trembling. "You okay? Look at me, Daisy."

Just as I tried to catch my breath, something cold and wet dripped onto my shoulder. I flinched, instinctively brushing at it, but it only smeared more of the liquid across my skin. "What the—"

Theo, standing beside me, reached out, his hand smeared with the substance. He rubbed it between his fingers and then held it up to the light. His face drained of color as the realization hit all of us at the same time—it was blood. Thick, warm blood.

We all looked up, our bodies moving in slow motion, as Maya shakily raised her phone toward the ceiling of the cave. The beam of light crawled over the jagged rocks until it landed on something dangling from a rusted metal rod embedded in the cave wall. The light flickered, casting eerie shadows across what was unmistakably a human body.

It hung there, limp and broken, swaying ever so slightly. The skin was torn, hanging loosely, and blood dripped down from its grotesquely stretched mouth. The intestines spilled out, coiling from the body and trailing down to the floor, still wet with fresh blood. One eye was missing from its socket, leaving a hollow, gaping wound where it should have been.

"Oh my God," I whispered, barely able to comprehend what I was seeing.

The body's single remaining eye stared back at us, lifeless, while the other—the one I had just held—now lay discarded on the cave floor. My knees felt weak, and the air in the cave seemed to thicken as if it were suffocating us with the horror of the scene.

Maya's face turned ghostly pale, her lips trembling as she covered her mouth, fighting back sobs. Eric stood frozen, his jaw clenched, eyes wide with a mix of terror and revulsion.

"What... what kind of place is this?" Maya whispered, her voice barely audible, as though speaking too loudly would make the nightmare even more real.

I swallowed hard, trying to keep my voice steady. "We... we have to get out of here."

As we bolted forward, hands gripping tightly together, the adrenaline in our veins gave us speed we didn't know we had.

Our footsteps pounded against the rocky ground, echoing in the hollow cave as we ran for what felt like five minutes straight. The darkness seemed to close in on us, but we kept going, driven by fear and desperation. Then, without warning, Eric came to a sudden stop.

Maya, panting, asked, "What's wrong? Why did you stop?"

Eric's face was pale, his eyes wide with a horrible realization. "What if... what if that body was Tristan?"

Theo and I exchanged a look, our breath catching. His eyes locked with mine, wide and terrified. My stomach churned. "No," I whispered, but my voice was shaky, hollow. "It can't be. It can't be Tristan."

Theo's reaction was immediate and violent. "No! No way, that's not Tristan!" His voice was frantic, louder with each word. He screamed again, almost as if trying to convince himself more than us. "It can't be him! It's not Tristan!"

Maya took a step back, shaking her head violently. "I can't go near that... thing. It's too much. Too horrible. I just... I can't," her voice broke, trembling with disgust and fear. "But it can't be Tristan. No. It can't."

Eric exhaled deeply, his face hardening with determination. "Stay here," he commanded, his voice steady despite the tension in the air. He turned to me and Maya. "I'll go check with Theo. If it's not him, we'll have peace. Just stay put."

"I... no, I can't!" I blurted, the words spilling out before I could stop them. "That's not Tristan. We need to leave—now!"

But Theo cut me off, his voice desperate, "I'm not going back until we know for sure! We can't leave without knowing."

Eric nodded, his jaw clenched, but there was something in his eyes—fear, tension—that told me he was barely holding it together. "Just one look, Daisy. One look. We all need to know the truth."

He reached for Maya, pulling her close, then grabbed my hand, his grip firm. "Stay strong. We'll face this together. No matter what we find."

The fear in his voice matched mine, but he wasn't giving in. Slowly, hesitantly, we moved toward the grotesque scene, each step making the dread in my chest tighten like a vise. The stench hit us first, overwhelming and rotten, but we pressed forward, hands covering our noses.

As we reached the body, my heart hammered painfully in my chest. I could hardly breathe.

Theo's voice was barely above a whisper as he turned toward the body. "Is... is that him?" His voice cracked, thick with emotion, as he stared at the mangled figure.

"I... I don't know," Eric muttered, his eyes wide with horror. "How can anyone know? It's too... too—" He trailed off, his words lost in the overwhelming disgust of the scene in front of us.

Just then, Maya, shaking uncontrollably, pointed a trembling finger toward the body's limp hand hanging down, the flesh torn and barely recognizable. "Look. The hand..." she whispered.

My eyes followed her gaze. My blood froze. A silver ring glinted faintly in the dim light. My vision blurred as I took a step back, my knees weak. "No! No!" I screamed, my voice hysterical, my heart tearing itself apart inside my chest. "No, that can't be!"

Eric rushed toward me, wrapping his arms around my shaking body, trying to calm me. "Daisy, stop. Please, calm down. What is it? What happened?"

I pointed with a trembling hand toward the ring. "That ring... that's the one I gave him. That's Tristan's ring! Oh God... it's him. It's Tristan!" My voice broke, and my world shattered.

Theo's face drained of all color as his eyes locked onto the ring. He stumbled backward, then collapsed to his knees. "No..." He gasped. "No, no, no!" His cries grew louder as he punched the ground, sobbing. "Tristan, no! It can't be you! It can't be you!"

He pounded his fists against the stone, his grief tearing through him like a storm.

Eric knelt beside Theo, his face full of pain as he placed a hand on Theo's shoulder. "Theo... Theo, please. Stay with us. We'll get through this. You have to stay strong. For him."

Maya stood frozen, her face pale and her hands trembling. I couldn't stop shaking, the cold, numb feeling spreading through my body like ice. I could barely register Maya as she rubbed my face, trying to bring me back, but everything felt distant, like a nightmare I couldn't wake from.

Eric's voice was low but steady, the only thing holding us together. "We're getting out of here," he said, his grip tightening around us. "All of us. Together."

Part 18 – Moonlit Descent

As we walked, flashes of Tristan and me swirled in my mind like fragments of a shattered memory. The sight of his lifeless body haunted every step. I tried to hold onto something real, something of him, but all I could picture was that horrible, mangled corpse. The Tristan I once knew was slipping away from me.

I stopped my voice barely a whisper. "Maya... can you show me his picture? Please, I can't remember him, not properly. All I can see is..." I trailed off, my voice breaking.

Maya glanced at me, her eyes filled with concern. "Daisy, now's not the time. We need to get out of here."

"Please," I begged, locking eyes with her, desperate to hold on to any piece of Tristan that wasn't drenched in blood. "Just one last time."

She hesitated, then sighed, knowing I wouldn't let it go. "There's barely any charge left on my phone," she said, but I could see the resolve in her eyes falter. She pulled out her phone anyway, quickly navigating to Instagram. When she finally opened the picture of Tristan, the sight of his face—alive and smiling—hit me like a punch to the gut.

But then she scrolled, and there it was: a picture of Tristan and his girlfriend from just a few weeks ago. They were together, beaming at the camera. The image blurred as tears welled up in my eyes. And just like that, the lines I'd written in my Artsy Diary, the ones I'd scrawled out in pain when I first found out about them, whispered through my mind, echoing in my ears:

"We were just kids when we fell in love, not knowing how it would end. I tried to hold on, but I lost you to her in the end. But you look perfect with her tonight."

Those words had once carried a depth I could barely fathom. Tristan had once sung "Perfect" by Ed Sheeran to me, his voice weaving a tapestry of emotions that felt unbreakable.

Back then, it was our song, a promise of what we thought we'd become together. I remembered the way his voice would soften whenever he sang it, how he'd smile at me as though nothing else mattered in the world.

But now... now that memory felt like a cruel joke. Tristan had moved on, found someone else. He had fallen in love again, and the song we shared was nothing more than an echo of a broken promise.

I stared at the picture of Tristan and his new girlfriend on Maya's phone, their smiling faces almost glowing under the dim light of the screen. His arm was draped casually around her shoulder, the same way he used to hold me. It was surreal, like I was looking at a version of him I never knew existed.

My mind struggled to reconcile the Tristan I remembered with the one in the photo.

I felt hollow. Everything that had once seemed special between us—his words, his touch, even that song—felt distant, as if they had belonged to someone else all along. My chest tightened, and the tears threatened to spill again.

How could I still hold onto him when he had let me go so easily?

It felt like the universe was mocking me. I clenched my fists, my heart aching as if it were being torn apart all over again.

At least he could've just lived with her happily when he finally got the one he deserved. I wanted to be angry—angry at him for moving on, angry at Sarah for being in the picture—but all I felt was a deep, suffocating sadness.

He should have been there, laughing, sharing moments that would fill his life with joy.

"Instead, he was just ashes of memory in both mine and Sarah's lives."

The thought twisted in my stomach like a knife. Tristan deserved happiness; we all did. And now, all I had left were fragments of a love that once burned so brightly. I remembered the laughter we shared, the dreams we whispered to each other late at night, and the hopes that we had for our future.

But now, those dreams lay scattered, like ashes in the wind, carried away by the reality that he was gone. I glanced at the photo again, my heart aching at the sight of his carefree smile. How could he look so happy when I was drowning in grief?

It was my mistake; I didn't make him feel satisfied when we were together.

I replayed every moment in my mind, every conversation that drifted into silence, every time I let my insecurities push him away. Later, I realized that "The distance between us was like sky and ocean—two beautiful elements that could never truly mix. No matter how much we tried, the gulf remained, vast and unbridgeable"

I should have fought harder, should have shown him how much he meant to me. But instead, I let him slip through my fingers, and now he was lost to me forever.

The darkness of the cave felt like it was closing in on me, mirroring the chaos inside my head.

The vivid memory of Tristan's laughter echoed in my mind, yet the picture in front of me was a reminder that I was left behind in a world that had moved on without me."Daisy, we have to go," Maya urged, her voice cutting through the fog of despair. "We can't stay here." Her words stirred something deep within me, a flicker of determination.

Maybe I couldn't hold on to Tristan, but I could hold on to the memories—those fleeting moments that made me feel alive. I took a deep breath, trying to steady myself, and nodded, ready to face whatever came next.

Eric stood near the cave entrance, his face lit with a mix of relief and excitement. "I see an exit! There's light up ahead!" he shouted, his voice echoing in the darkness. I could see the glimmer in his eyes, a flicker of hope that felt almost contagious.

But even as his words reached us, I couldn't shake the feeling that we were just avoiding the gravity of what we had witnessed. Maya nodded, still gripping my arm tightly. "Yeah, we're coming!" she called back, her voice steadier than I felt.

As we stumbled out of the cave, the cool night air enveloped us, a stark contrast to the stifling darkness we had just escaped.

It was nearly midnight, but the moon hung high in the sky, casting a silver glow over everything.

The waterfall sparkled like a cascade of stars, illuminated by the moon's reflection, creating an ethereal beauty that felt surreal against the horrors we had left behind.

For a moment, the sight took my breath away. I wanted to savor the tranquility, to believe we were free from the nightmare inside. But in my heart, I knew the truth—we were still haunted by what we had found.

The beauty of the night felt like a cruel joke, juxtaposed against the darkness we carried within.

Part 19 - Together in the Unknown

Theo couldn't stop crying for Tristan. His sobs echoed through the quiet night as Eric knelt beside him, trying his best to calm him. Meanwhile, Maya didn't leave my hand, not for a moment, holding on as though she feared I might vanish too.

The moon above us seemed eerie, casting its pale light over the landscape. Its glow felt cold, as if it knew the weight of Tristan's death. It hung like a silent witness to everything, the same moon he once looked up at, never knowing his end would come like this.

Suddenly, Maya's phone died, the screen flickering off and leaving us in near darkness. We were without signal already, and now, without light. The torch was gone. I gasped at the thought of being completely cut off. Our shoes were caked in dirt and mud, thick and wet from the cave's passage, but it felt like more than that—like the weight of everything pressing down on us.

"Sarah... why would she kill him?" Eric's voice cut through the stillness, his tone filled with confusion that matched the puzzle pieces in our minds.

Theo paused his crying, wiping his nose with his sleeve. "Do you think she did it?" he asked, still shaken.

"No," Eric replied, but there was hesitation. "But it does feel like a puzzle... Daisy found her bracelet. There was that note, and now she's left her house too. Feels like she's running."

Maya, her voice uncertain but sharp, added, "If Sarah did this... we can get out of here too. She's not brave. I've seen her pictures—she looks fragile, like someone who would break at the smallest touch."

Eric gave her a hard look. "Weak people sometimes turn strong when they've been pushed too far. Maybe that's what happened here."

Maya continued, her brow furrowed, "But why did Tristan still have the ring you gave him, Daisy? Even after he was with Sarah"

Did I... did I make them break up?"

I made them leave each other," I muttered, the guilt heavy in my chest. The thought gnawed at me, that maybe I had been the reason everything fell apart.

Eric walked towards me, leaving Theo for a moment. He stood in front of me, his eyes serious but filled with warmth. "Daisy, don't think like that. It's Tristan. You didn't come between him and Sarah. We don't know what really happened." He paused, his voice lowering. "But whatever it was, you're not to blame."

I shook my head, anger bubbling up inside me. "Stop, Eric. I made him leave. I pushed him away. Poor Tristan... he went through so much. He used to take sleeping pills just to get through the night. I broke him." My voice wavered, filled with the pain of old memories.

Maya sighed, her tone softer but still honest. "That's one side of it. But Daisy, you were hurt too. Should I tell Eric and Theo about your pain? About what you went through when you were together?"

I clenched my teeth, my heart aching from the reminder of how much I had been struggling.

Theo spoke up, his voice still fragile but steadying. "Both of you were hurt. It's about building each other back up, not tearing each other down."

Eric nodded in agreement, standing tall beside me. "Look, Daisy, when you had trouble communicating with him, Tristan should've understood. He should've been there for you. But instead, he left."

I snapped back, my voice breaking. "No, he didn't leave! I left... because I thought I was giving him pain. I hurt him."

Eric stared at me, his voice firm yet gentle. "When you left, did Tristan try to come after you? Did he ask for you back?"

I glanced at Maya, who shook her head. "No, he didn't. He didn't even come after her. That's what hurt Daisy the most... she expected him to try, but he never did."

Eric's face hardened with understanding. "He should have come. Men, when they love someone, don't just let them go. It's not about who's wrong. Tristan... he let you slip away, Daisy."

There was a long pause as we stood there, the weight of Eric's words sinking in. I could feel Maya's hand trembling in mine, Theo's quiet sobs and the coldness of the moon watching us from above. And for the first time, the guilt didn't feel so overwhelming.

Maya glanced around, her expression tight with concern. "We can't stay here for long. Soon it's going to get colder, and we need to find shelter."

Eric shook his head, frustrated. "There's no shelter in these woods. And we can't risk getting more lost."

Maya's words barely registered before I felt a wave of nausea rise from my stomach. The awful stench of the cave, the dirt caking my shoes, and the weight of everything finally overwhelmed me. I turned away quickly, vomiting onto the ground.

I felt Maya's hand gently on my back, her touch steady and reassuring as she knelt beside me.

"It's okay, just breathe," she whispered. Theo quickly passed a handkerchief to Maya, who wiped my mouth with care. "You're alright. We've got you," she said, her voice soft, her fingers brushing the hair away from my face as she tried to comfort me.

As I wiped my eyes, Eric came closer. Without a word, he took off his shirt and draped it over my shoulders, his expression full of concern. "You'll feel warmer this way," he said quietly, his gaze meeting mine for a moment, filled with something that felt like protection like he couldn't stand to see me hurt.

Theo Whispered, "If Tristan were here, he'd probably scold you for pushing yourself so hard," he tried to joke, though his voice wavered with emotion.

Eric's brow furrowed. "Tristan didn't always show enough love or care, even when he was with Daisy. Why do you think—"

"Stop it!" Maya cut him off, standing up sharply. "This isn't the time to be at each other's throats. We're all lost and hurt. Let's focus on getting through this." She turned to me, her expression softening as she offered her hand to help me stand.

Theo rose, taking a deep breath. "I'll go and check if I can find shelter nearby," he said. "We can't stay out here in the cold."

"I'll look in the opposite direction," Eric added, stepping toward the woods.

I grabbed his arm, my voice shaky. "We can't split up. How can you guys even think about leaving us alone out here?"

Theo shook his head, glancing at Eric, but before he could respond, Maya quickly chimed in. "No, Daisy, you go with Eric. I'll join Theo."

I narrowed my eyes at her. Maya was being clever, playing the good friend card, but I knew what she was doing. She knew about the tension between Eric and me, and she was trying to push us together. She always knew how to read the situation, even when things were at their worst.

"No one's splitting up," I insisted, my voice firm despite the fear gnawing at me. "After everything that just happened with Theo, we can't risk it. We're sticking together."

Eric squeezed my hand gently, his thumb brushing over my knuckles again. "Daisy's right. We can't split up. Not after all this. We'll face whatever's out there as one. We're safer together."

Theo sighed, looking between us all. "Alright, we stick together then, but we need to find shelter soon."

The atmosphere was tense, the weight of what had just happened still pressing down on all of us. But at least we weren't alone. And as we walked forward, I held on to the small hope that somehow, together, we'd make it through.

PART 20 - THE LIGHT OF HOPE

We all walked together, the thick, damp air clinging to our skin as we trudged through the forest. The once comforting sounds of rustling leaves and distant chirping were now unnerving, amplified by the darkness that seemed to stretch on forever. It was hard to keep our minds off the situation—what we had seen, what had happened to Tristan, and the suffocating fear that we might not make it out of here.

As we walked, Theo broke the silence. "Do you think Tristan knew... knew this would happen?"

His voice was low, filled with sorrow and guilt. "I feel like there were signs, you know?"

Eric scoffed, his tone sharper than it should have been. "Signs? Like what? He didn't tell anyone if there were."

Theo's steps faltered, and he spun around to face Eric. "You think I don't feel guilty enough, Eric? You think I didn't see him struggling?"

Eric shook his head, clearly frustrated. "I'm not blaming you, but what's done is done. We need to focus on getting out of here alive."

Theo clenched his fists, and for a moment, I thought they might actually start fighting. The tension between them was thick, their shared pain surfacing in bursts of anger. But just as quickly, Eric sighed, rubbing the back of his neck.

"I'm sorry, Theo," Eric muttered. "We're all hurting. It's just—this whole thing, it's messing with my head."

Theo's shoulders relaxed a little, and he nodded. "I know. I'm sorry too."

They exchanged a brief look, one of understanding. Whatever anger had flared between them, it was quenched by their shared determination to survive.

After an hour of walking, the conversation shifted to survival. "Remember those evenings when we'd find fruits on our way back from the waterfall?" Maya said, her voice tinged with nostalgia. "Now, we can't even see if there are any fruits hanging on the trees."

"Yeah," Eric sighed. "It's like nature's turned against us. If we don't get out of these woods soon, we're going to starve."

My stomach growled at the thought, a painful reminder that we hadn't eaten anything for hours. The hunger was gnawing at all of us, and the fear of not finding anything to eat was starting to sink in.

As we walked further, we came across a small river. The water glistened under the moonlight, a calm in the middle of our chaos. It wasn't more than three feet deep, and as we prepared to cross it, Eric suddenly stopped, his eyes lighting up with an idea.

"How about we eat fish tonight?" he said, his voice suddenly filled with hope.

"Fish? Seriously?" I raised an eyebrow.

"Impossible," Theo added. "We don't have anything to catch them with."

Eric ignored our skepticism and turned to Maya. "Hey, Maya, that cardigan you're wearing. It's netted, right?"

Maya blinked, looking down at the thin cardigan she had on. "Yeah... Why?"

Eric grinned. "We can use it as a net. Tie it between two sticks, and boom, instant fishing gear."

Maya stared at him in disbelief. "That's my favorite cardigan, Eric!"

He shrugged, grabbing two long sticks from the ground. "If we get out of this forest alive, I'll buy you a hundred cardigans. But right now, we need to survive."

Maya groaned but didn't protest further as she took off the cardigan, her face showing reluctance as she handed it over to Eric. "You owe me a new one."

"Deal." Eric swiftly tied the cardigan between the sticks, forming a makeshift net.

To our surprise, it worked. After a few attempts, Eric managed to scoop up two small fish from the river. Maya screamed when she saw the fish wriggling in the net, but Eric just laughed.

"Dinner is served," he said, holding the fish up triumphantly.

"Unbelievable," Theo muttered, shaking his head but with a hint of a smile.

The momentary victory lifted our spirits, but as we sat by the river, preparing to make a small fire, the weight of our situation still loomed large. The forest was unforgiving, and we had a long way to go before we'd see safety again.

Maya sighed, sitting next to me, her voice softer now. "We're not out of this yet, are we?"

I glanced at Eric, who was focused on the fish, and Theo, who sat quietly, lost in thought. "No," I replied, my voice barely a whisper. "But we're together, and that's something."

The fish tasted better than expected, sizzling on the small fire Eric managed to build. We savored every bite, but it didn't fully satisfy our aching hunger. It was enough to keep us going for a while longer, though.

We continued walking, the woods stretching endlessly before us, the darkness now almost comforting in its familiarity. Our conversation drifted between fragments of memories and plans, trying to distract ourselves from the gnawing fear that still lingered.

Then, in the distance, a faint glow appeared. It flickered like a beacon through the trees, causing Maya to freeze in her tracks. "Do you see that?" she whispered, her voice trembling with a mix of fear and hope.

Eric and Theo didn't hesitate. They grabbed our hands and ran toward the light, our hearts pounding with anticipation. As we got closer, we realized it was a house.

"A house? In the middle of the woods?" I asked, breathless from both the running and the disbelief.

Maya looked at me, her brow furrowed in confusion. "No way. Eric, Theo, is this your villa?" Eric's brow furrowed, shaking his head. "What? No. Our villa is on the other side of the city. This looks nothing like it."

I gave him a knowing glance. "You're telling me you have only one villa in this city?"

Eric shrugged. "We have many, but this one isn't ours."

The house loomed before us, shadowed by tall trees and overgrown bushes, yet strangely inviting with its lights on. We hesitated, standing in the backyard, hearts lighter at the thought of shelter but wary of what might be inside.

"If it's empty, why are the lights on?" I asked, suspicion creeping into my voice.

Maya crossed her arms. "They're rich enough to not care about electricity. Rich people don't bother about such things. They leave the lights on to keep animals away. Animals don't attack brightly lit places."

Theo snorted as he examined a window, running his fingers along the sill. "Brainless. What's the point of fancy locks and windows if anyone can just break in? See?" He jimmied the window open effortlessly.

Eric chuckled. "Maybe someone is inside. Be careful."

"I don't think so," Maya said, glancing around. "I don't see anyone."

We hesitated for a moment longer, but eventually, curiosity and exhaustion won out. One by one, we climbed in through the window. Maya headed straight for the kitchen, while Theo and Eric moved cautiously around the house, checking for any signs of life.

After a few minutes, we relaxed. It was clear there was no one here. The house was eerily quiet, but it felt like a refuge, a place we could finally breathe. I wandered upstairs, following the dim light to a small room where I found a charging station. My heart leaped.

"Guys!" I called down, excitement rising. "Come upstairs! There's a wireless charging station!"We hurriedly placed our phones on the chargers, watching the little battery icons light up with a relief that was short-lived. No network.

I sighed, frustrated, as the others headed back downstairs. "I'll be down soon," I said. "Just need to freshen up."

Alone, I opened my phone, and there it was—Tristan's face, his smiling photo still set as my wallpaper. My chest tightened, the sorrow rushing back like a tidal wave. Seeing his face felt like a knife twisting in my gut.

We had Wi-Fi, but without the password, it was useless. The hope of connecting to the outside world faded as quickly as it had come. I opened my WhatsApp, scrolling aimlessly until I came across his chat.

"Once, we spoke every day, lost in endless scrolls of time, Now, all that's left lies quiet, buried in the archive"

The words hit me like a punch, the realization crashing down. His messages, the ones I used to cling to, were now nothing but relics of a past that no longer mattered.

Suddenly, a scream shattered the silence—Maya's scream.

I bolted downstairs, heart racing. Something was wrong.

PART 21 - WOODS OF HUNGER

As I rushed downstairs, my heart pounded in my chest, the eerie silence of the house amplifying Maya's scream. I stumbled down the last few steps, my mind racing with possibilities—had someone come back? Was there an intruder?

When I burst into the room, I found Maya standing near the kitchen, her face pale, eyes wide in shock. Theo and Eric were beside her, looking just as confused.

"What happened?" I asked, my voice trembling.

Maya pointed to the ground. "I... I saw something moving, right there!" Her hand shook as she gestured toward a corner of the room. "I swear it was like a shadow, but it disappeared before I could get a proper look."

Eric immediately rushed over, squatting down to inspect the area. He ran his fingers across the floor, feeling for any disturbance, but came up empty. "There's nothing here, Maya. Maybe it was just your mind playing tricks on you after everything we've been through."

Maya shook her head furiously. "No, it wasn't my imagination. I saw it. Something was there."Theo let out a deep breath, trying to steady himself after the scare. "Look, this place is creepy as hell. Let's not jump to conclusions just yet. But we need to be cautious. We don't know what's out there—or in here."

Eric stood up, his eyes scanning the room for any other signs of movement. "Alright, let's check this house thoroughly. We're not taking any risks."

We split up, with Theo and Eric taking one side of the house while Maya and I stuck together. My stomach was still unsettled from earlier, and the faint echo of Tristan's face on my phone screen still lingered in my mind, along with the unsettling feeling of being watched. The more we explored, the more I couldn't shake the thought that we weren't alone.

As we walked through the narrow hallways, Maya whispered, "This place gives me the creeps. Who just leaves a house like this in the middle of nowhere? And why are the lights on?"

I nodded, my throat tight. "I don't know... but it doesn't feel right. Something about this place feels... off."

We made our way toward what looked like an old study. The air felt heavy as if the very walls held secrets we were not meant to uncover. Maya opened the door cautiously, and as we stepped inside, a faint smell of dust and mildew hit us. The room was lined with bookshelves, and in the middle, an old desk sat, untouched by time.

Maya walked over to the desk and reached for a drawer. "Let's see if there's anything useful in here."

She pulled it open, and we both froze. Inside the drawer, nestled among papers and old notebooks, was a photograph. Maya carefully lifted it out and turned it toward me. It was Tristan.

My heart skipped a beat. "What... how is that here?"

Maya's hand trembled as she stared at the photo, her voice barely a whisper. "This can't be real..."

Eric and Theo entered the room just then, their expressions hardening as they saw the photo in Maya's hand.

"What the hell is that doing here?" Eric demanded, walking toward us.

I stared at the picture, a chill running down my spine. Tristan's familiar smile stared back at me, but there was something wrong. His eyes looked different—darker, more hollow. And then I noticed the date in the corner.

"This was taken after... after he disappeared," I said, my voice shaky.

Theo's face paled. "That's impossible. How could anyone have this?"

Eric reached for the photo, his hands shaking slightly. "This doesn't make any sense."

Maya bit her lip, her eyes darting nervously between us. "We need to get out of here. This house... something's not right."

Theo nodded, his voice barely audible. "Agreed. But we can't leave without knowing what's going on. This place—it's connected to Tristan somehow."

I took a deep breath, my head spinning with questions and fear. "Whatever this is... we have to be careful. We're not alone here."

And with that, the weight of Tristan's shadow grew heavier over us, as if the house itself was alive, watching, waiting for us to uncover its darkest secret.

As the eerie silence settled around us after discovering the photo of Tristan, a deep unease filled the room. I glanced between the faces of my friends—Eric tense with frustration, Theo pale and still, and Maya clutching the photograph like it was a lifeline to reality. We needed to get out of here, but the photo held us captive, as if answering the call of the dead.

Eric finally spoke, his voice rough. "We need to move. Staying here isn't safe."

"What if there's more?" Theo asked, his voice wavering. "More photos... more signs?"Eric shot him a sharp look. "You want to stay here longer? After what we've already been through?"

I looked back at the photo, trying to understand how it could exist. Tristan looked like he had been alive, well after we lost him, but his eyes... they were hollow, empty. It sent shivers down my spine.

Theo shifted nervously. "Maybe... maybe we should look upstairs. Maybe there's something that'll explain why this is here."

Maya looked at Theo like he'd lost his mind. "Theo, no. We need to get out. We found the photo—now we leave. I'm not about to spend another second in this creepy house."

Eric's hand tightened around the photo. "I agree with Maya. We leave now. This place feels wrong, and whatever happened to Tristan... we can't solve it by staying in this house."

I swallowed hard, feeling the weight of everything bearing down on me. The moment had become too much. "I... I don't know. Maybe Theo's right. What if we miss something that could help us figure out what happened to him?"

Eric sighed, rubbing his temples. "Daisy... look, I understand. But we're not detectives. We're in over our heads. Staying here is just asking for trouble."

The tension between Theo and Eric thickened. Theo's eyes burned with frustration. "We can't just run away every time it gets tough! Tristan is dead, and we don't even know why! If there's a clue in this house, we owe it to him to find it."

Eric stepped closer to Theo, his voice low but seething. "We've been through hell tonight. You think a clue is worth risking our lives?"

I could see the anger in both of them building, ready to explode. Maya stepped in between them, her voice calm but firm. "Stop. This isn't the time to fight. We need to stay together. We're all scared, but we can't turn on each other now."

Eric took a step back, exhaling sharply. "Fine. But we need a plan."

Just then, a strange creaking sound echoed through the house, as if something—or someone—was moving above us. We all froze, our eyes wide with terror.

Maya's grip on my arm tightened. "What was that?"

Theo's face hardened, determination flickering in his eyes. "That's it. We need to check upstairs. There's something up there."

Eric shook his head, his face pale. "No way. We leave. Now."

But Theo was already heading for the staircase, his footsteps echoing against the old wooden floor. Maya looked at me, fear clouding her eyes, but there was something else—an unspoken understanding.

"Are we really doing this?" she asked, her voice a mix of disbelief and fear.

I nodded, despite the pounding in my chest. "We can't leave without knowing."

Eric's shoulders slumped in defeat as he followed behind. "You guys are insane."

With every step we took up the narrow staircase, the air felt thicker, like the house itself was watching us, drawing us closer to some dark secret it had kept hidden for far too long.

When we reached the landing, Theo paused, staring down a long hallway. "Whatever's here... we'll find it. Just stay close."

We moved down the hall, passing by doors that looked un-touched for years, the air growing colder. The final door at the end of the hall creaked open slowly, as if beckoning us inside.

Theo was the first to step in, followed by Maya, then Eric. I hesitated, my heart pounding so hard it hurt. But I forced myself to follow them.

Inside, there was nothing but dust and old furniture. It looked like an ordinary room—until I saw the writing on the wall.

Scrawled in messy, jagged letters, barely visible in the dim light, were the words:_"He didn't die... we took him."_

Maya gasped, backing up into me. Eric cursed under his breath. Theo stood frozen, his eyes locked on the words.

"What does that even mean?" Maya whispered, her voice trembling.

"I don't know," I said, my voice just as shaky. "But whatever it is, it's not over. Tristan's death... there's something more."

Eric turned to us, his eyes dark with realization. "We need to leave. Now."

But before we could move, we heard a loud thud from somewhere in the house below.We weren't alone.

The thud echoed through the house, freezing us in place. We all exchanged panicked glances. Maya's hand flew to her mouth, trying to stifle a gasp, while Theo's face drained of color.

"What was that?" Maya whispered, her voice trembling.

Eric took a deep breath, his eyes darting toward the doorway. "Stay calm. We don't know what it was. It could've been the wind or something falling over."

"Wind doesn't make a noise like that," I muttered, my voice tight with fear. "It sounded like... like someone is here."

Theo looked back at the writing on the wall, his jaw clenched. "We're not alone. Whoever wrote that... they're still here."

Eric stepped forward, trying to assert control. "Alright, listen. We need to stay together. We can't just freak out and make rash decisions."

"Too late," Maya whispered under her breath, her eyes wide as she clung to my arm.

Theo took a step toward the door, his fists clenched at his sides. "I'm not waiting around for whatever made that sound to come to us. We need to find a way out."

I looked at Eric, pleading with my eyes. "Please, let's go. We shouldn't be here. It's not safe."

He nodded, swallowing hard. "We're leaving. Now."

We all moved quickly toward the door, but just as we reached the threshold, another thud came from downstairs—louder this time, closer. My heart felt like it was going to burst from my chest as my mind raced with all the possibilities of what—or who—was making that noise.

Eric gestured for us to stay behind him, his eyes hard with determination. "I'll go first. Stay close."

We descended the stairs slowly, every creak of the old wooden steps making my stomach twist tighter with fear. As we reached the bottom, I could feel the weight of the house bearing down on us, like it was alive and aware of our presence.

Theo gripped the railing tightly, his knuckles white. "This place... it's not right."

Maya let out a shaky breath. "No kidding. We need to get out of here before—"

Suddenly, the front door burst open, slamming against the wall with a deafening crash.

We all screamed, instinctively backing away as a figure stepped through the doorway. The dim light from the outside barely illuminated them, casting long shadows that stretched across the room.

For a split second, I thought it was Tristan—somehow alive, returning to confront us. But as the figure stepped into the light, I realized it wasn't him.

It was a man. Older, rugged, with a worn face and wild eyes. He looked like he hadn't seen civilization in years.

"Who... who are you?" Eric demanded, his voice shaking with both fear and anger.

The man didn't answer right away. His eyes scanned the room, taking in the sight of us, the writing on the wall, and the chaos we had left in our wake. Then, he spoke, his voice rough like gravel.

"You shouldn't be here."

Theo took a step forward, trying to assert himself. "We're just passing through. We didn't mean to trespass."

The man's eyes flicked to Theo, narrowing. "You think this is just some abandoned house? You think you can just walk in and take whatever you want?"

"No, we didn't take anything," Maya said quickly, her voice high-pitched with fear. "We just... we just wanted to find out what happened to our friend."

The man's gaze turned cold. "Your friend? You think he was the first? You think this is about one boy?"

My heart stilled. "What... what do you mean?"

He took a step closer, and I instinctively moved back, bumping into Eric, who put a protective arm around me.

"You need to leave," the man growled. "This place... it's cursed. The woods, the caves... they take people. And once they do, there's no coming back."

Eric, ever the skeptic, clenched his jaw. "That's just some local legend. We don't believe in that."

The man's expression darkened. "You don't have to believe it for it to be real."

Theo's voice was a low growl. "Are you saying Tristan...?"

The man's eyes glinted in the dim light. "I'm saying you need to get out while you still can. Before the woods take you too."

Panic surged through me. "What do you mean the woods take people?"

The man stepped closer, his voice dropping to a harsh whisper. "The woods have their own hunger. They draw you in with false promises, like shelter and safety. But once you're inside, you're theirs."

Maya let out a small, terrified gasp. "This can't be real. This isn't happening."

Eric squared his shoulders, his voice trembling but firm. "We're leaving now."

The man nodded, his eyes never leaving ours. "Go. And don't come back. Whatever took your friend... it's not finished yet."

We bolted for the door, the fear of the unknown propelling us forward as we ran out of the house and into the cold night. I could feel my heart hammering in my chest, every step bringing us closer to the edge of panic.But as we fled into the woods, the man's final words echoed in my mind, chilling me to the core.It wasn't finished yet.

Part 22 - Beneath the Surface of Deceit

We sprinted through the woods, the crunch of leaves and branches beneath our feet as loud as our labored breaths. The darkness pressed in around us, the moonlight barely filtering through the thick canopy of trees. My heart pounded, not just from running, but from the fear gnawing at the edges of my mind.

Maya held my hand tightly, her nails digging into my skin. Eric and Theo were ahead, their forms barely visible in the dim light as we followed the narrow path.

I couldn't shake the man's words from my head. The woods have their own hunger. It sounded ridiculous, like something out of a ghost story, but the eerie feeling of being watched clung to me.

After what felt like an eternity, Eric slowed down, hands on his knees, gasping. "We need to stop... for a minute," he panted.

Theo paced, his face pale and tight with tension. "That guy was insane. We should've never gone near that place."

Maya let out a shaky breath, eyes darting around. "Do you think... do you think he was right? About the woods?"

Eric straightened, his jaw hardening. "No. He's just some crazy old man. We'll get out, and everything will be fine."

But I wasn't so sure. The woods felt darker now, oppressive. It felt like the trees themselves were closing in on us. I tried to push it aside, but the weight lingered.

"We need to keep moving," I whispered. "We can't stay here."

Theo nodded. "She's right. Let's go."

We walked again, slower, exhaustion pressing down on us. The silence in the woods was eerie, no wildlife, just our footsteps. Every now and then, I glanced at Eric, who gave me a nod, though tension carved into his face.

Suddenly, Theo stopped. "Do you hear that?" he whispered, eyes wide.

We all froze, listening. At first, I heard nothing, but then... there it was. A faint, rhythmic sound, like footsteps but wrong.

It was behind us.

Eric's face tightened. "We're not alone."

Maya whimpered, gripping me tighter. "What do we do?"

"Keep moving," Eric said quickly, his voice low. "Don't run. Just walk."

We walked faster, but the sound followed, louder with each step. My heart raced. After a few minutes, the sound stopped. We froze, glancing around, but nothing moved. Just the trees, darkness, and the silence.

"Maybe it was just an animal," Maya whispered, trembling.

Theo shook his head. "That wasn't an animal."

Suddenly, we saw it—a faint glow ahead. Hope surged. Maybe a clearing, or even a cave for shelter.

Without a word, we ran toward the light. It grew brighter, until we saw a large cave, its mouth faintly illuminated from some hidden source. It felt strange, like a natural refuge, but also unsettling.

"We should stop here," Theo suggested, peering into the cave.

Eric hesitated, glancing at me. "We don't know what's inside, but we don't have many options."

As we stepped inside, the cave was eerily silent, the air cool and still. It wasn't exactly comforting, but it was safer than being out in the woods. We found a flat spot near the back of the cave and settled down.

"I'll keep watch," Eric said. "Just in case."

I wasn't sure I could sleep, but I was exhausted. As the others tried to rest, I leaned back against the cold stone wall, the unease still twisting inside me.

After a while, Maya stood up, her movements slow, her face pale. "I'll be back. I'm going to the toilet."

I frowned, glancing at her. "Now?"

She didn't meet my eyes. "Yeah. I won't be long."

Something about her tone didn't sit right with me, but before I could press, she was already walking away.

Minutes passed, and when Eric and Theo noticed she hadn't returned, concern flashed in their eyes. "We should check on her," Eric said. "It's risky for her to go alone, especially out here."

I agreed. Without hesitation, I retraced Maya's steps, my stomach twisting with worry.

As I hurried down the path, I spotted something strange—Maya descending into an open vent in the ground. She was moving quickly, as though she knew exactly where she was headed. My blood chilled, and instinctively, I followed her.

I crept down into the vent, trying to keep my breath steady. The air was damp, the walls narrow as I made my way down a set of stone steps. My heart pounded, and I could hear the faintest echo of voices ahead.

As I reached the bottom, the passage opened up into something much larger. My breath caught in my throat. It was an underground cabin, large and sprawling, with wooden beams and flickering lanterns casting long shadows across the floor. It was eerie, like something out of a nightmare.

I pressed myself behind a large crate near the entrance, my heart thundering as I caught sight of Maya. She was standing over someone—Sarah. Sarah's hands were tied behind her back, her face pale and streaked with dirt.

Maya's voice was low, but filled with fury. "How dare you try to leave?" she snarled, her hand gripping Sarah's throat. "You think you can just walk out of here?"Sarah whimpered, struggling against her bonds. "Maya, please... I didn't—"

Maya's voice cut through the air, sharp and venomous. "I told you, I have people watching you. You think I don't know what you're trying to do? You've already ruined enough. I won't let you destroy everything I've built."

I stayed frozen behind the crate, my breath shallow as I listened.

"You tried to make it look like I killed Tristan," Sarah gasped, her voice barely a whisper.

Maya laughed coldly, tightening her grip. "I didn't just try. I succeeded. Everyone thinks you did it, Sarah. They'll never believe it was me. I even planted his ring on that body in the cave. The cops won't question it."

My mind reeled. Maya framed Sarah... for Tristan's death?

Maya leaned in closer to Sarah, her voice a deadly whisper. "You're not getting out of here. And if you try, I'll make sure you regret it."

Sarah's eyes filled with terror as she struggled to speak. "You won't get away with this."

Maya sneered, her eyes glinting in the dim light. "I already have."

Chills ran down my spine as I crouched lower behind the crate. I couldn't believe what I was hearing. Maya... she did it. She killed Tristan.

And she had framed Sarah to take the fall.

I had to get out. I had to warn the others.

My heart raced as I crouched lower behind the crate, every nerve in my body screaming at me to get out. But I couldn't move, not yet. Not when Sarah's life was hanging by a thread, not when I knew Maya was capable of so much more than I had ever imagined.

Maya stood over Sarah, her expression cold, calculating. "You're going to stay down here, where you belong. No one's coming to save you."

I tried to steady my breath, inching backward, careful not to make a sound. I needed to get to Eric and Theo—warn them before Maya realized I'd followed her. But as I took a step, my foot brushed against something metallic. A soft clink echoed through the underground room.

Maya's head snapped toward the sound, her eyes narrowing. My blood ran cold.

"What was that?" she hissed, her voice sharp.

I pressed myself deeper behind the crate, holding my breath. Sarah's eyes darted toward the noise, but she remained silent, fear evident in her gaze.

Maya let go of Sarah and took a step toward where I was hiding, her eyes scanning the dimly lit room. "Is someone there?"

I froze, every muscle tense, praying she wouldn't see me. The lantern light flickered across the walls, casting long, eerie shadows. I could hear my heartbeat pounding in my ears, louder than anything else.

Maya took another step, her breath shallow, her eyes darting around. "If anyone's here, you won't make it out alive."

Panic surged through me, but I forced myself to stay still. She was so close now, I could feel her presence, her anger radiating off her in waves.

Suddenly, a noise from deeper in the underground chamber caught Maya's attention—a faint creak, like a door opening. She turned abruptly, her attention pulled away from me. I didn't wait for her to come back. I stood frozen behind the crate, my breath shallow as Maya scanned the room, eyes sharp and searching. My heart pounded in my chest as I stayed perfectly still, hoping the shadows and the flickering lantern light would keep me hidden. Maya's gaze swept over my hiding spot, but she didn't see me.

She turned back to Sarah, grabbing her roughly by the collar. "I'll be back soon," she hissed, her voice dripping with venom. "Don't even think about trying to escape. You know what happens if you do."

Sarah didn't speak, her eyes hollow and tired, but when Maya finally let her go, there was a quiet strength in her posture. Maya stepped back, brushing the dirt from her hands. "Goodbye, Sarah. Stay put, or there will be consequences."

Maya shot one last glance around the room, still suspicious, before turning on her heel and walking away. I watched her leave, her footsteps fading into the darkness of the underground passage. As soon as she was out of sight, I risked a glance toward Sarah.

Sarah's eyes met mine from across the room. There was no shock, no surprise—just a quiet warning in her gaze, as if she was telling me not to follow. Her expression wasn't fear; it was something deeper, a silent plea for my safety. Don't stay here. Run.

I nodded to her, a silent promise, then turned and slipped out of the passageway, back into the night. My heart raced as I moved, trying to make as little noise as possible. The darkness of the forest surrounded me again, but this time I could feel the weight of what I had witnessed. I had to get back to Eric and Theo, but I couldn't let Maya know that I'd followed her.

I picked up the pace, darting through the trees, my breath ragged as I pushed myself to move faster. Sweat trickled down my forehead, and I wiped it away with a shaky hand. Just as I reached the edge of the cave, I saw them—Eric, Theo, and Maya, all waiting, the flicker of the campfire casting eerie shadows on their faces.

Eric's eyes lit up when he saw me. "You're back! Where did you go? You went after Maya, but she came back a while ago."

I slowed my pace, forcing a calm expression even though my insides were still twisting with everything I had just seen. "I... I had to go to the toilet too," I said, keeping my voice steady. "And then I just wanted a bit of space to think, so I wandered nearby for a moment."

Theo raised an eyebrow, but he didn't question me further. Maya, however, moved toward me, her eyes softening in an unsettling way. She reached out and took my hand, her grip firm but not aggressive. "Don't ever do that again," she said, her voice low and filled with something almost like concern. "It's dangerous out here, and we need to stay together. It's harmful to wander off alone."

I nodded, my throat dry, unable to meet her gaze for too long. Then, to my surprise, Maya's expression shifted slightly, her fingers tightening around mine as if she was... apologizing. "I'm sorry, too," she murmured. "I shouldn't have worried you like that."

There was something in her tone—something off. But I couldn't dwell on it now. I gave a weak smile, pretending to accept her words, even as my heart continued to race with the truth I now held.

Part 23 - Betrayal Ticks Within

All I could think of were Maya's words to Sarah: "I even planted his ring on that body in the cave. The cops won't question it." It echoed over and over in my mind, chilling me to the bone. So, the body wasn't Tristan. That meant... was he still alive? Or had Maya hidden him somewhere? I had no idea how far her web of deception stretched. The thought of her watching Sarah—having people watch her—made it all the more disturbing. How was she even doing that?

Before I could spiral further into my thoughts, Theo broke the silence. "Let's sleep," he said softly, his voice heavy with exhaustion. It sounded simple, but I felt the tension in the air, thick like the forest around us.

Maya's hand slipped into mine, her grip gentle, but something in the gesture made my skin crawl. It wasn't just the touch. It was the watch on her wrist. As she held my hand, I noticed a faint light pulsing from under the face of the watch. I blinked, trying not to make my curiosity obvious. The more I looked, the more I realized it wasn't an ordinary watch. There was no ticking, no hands moving like an analog watch. I didn't dare ask

Maya what it was, but something about it felt wrong. Too sleek, too precise.

We lay down, and one by one, the others drifted into an uneasy sleep. But I couldn't close my eyes. The more I thought about that watch, the more unsettled I felt. What was it really? My mind raced with possibilities, each one darker than the last. Was this how she was watching people? Or was it something else entirely?

I waited until Maya's breathing deepened, signaling she was asleep. Then, ever so slowly, I leaned closer to her wrist. The faint glow from the watch was still there, flickering softly. I had to know.

With trembling fingers, I reached for it, moving slowly so as not to wake her. My hand hovered just above the surface, but nothing happened. I frowned, confused. It didn't seem like I could touch it, as if something was stopping me. I tried again, but the watch remained unresponsive, the glow mocking me in its stillness.

Frustrated, I paused and thought. Maya wasn't careless; she wouldn't wear something like this unless it had a purpose. Maybe there was a way to wake it up, a specific way it operated.

Then it hit me. What if it wasn't about physical touch? What if it responded to movement, sound, or... maybe heat?

Taking a deep breath, I rubbed my thumb and index finger together, trying to generate warmth. Slowly, I hovered my hand just above the watch again, but this time, as I held it closer, the faint glow pulsed brighter, reacting to the heat. My pulse quickened. I was onto something.

I brought my hand even closer, the warmth radiating from my fingers touching the surface of the watch. Suddenly, the glow intensified, and the face of the watch shifted. The smooth surface rippled like water, and I saw what looked like symbols flash briefly before the face went dark again.

What was that?

My heart pounded in my chest as I pulled my hand back. Whatever the watch was, it wasn't just for telling time. There was more to it—something deeply hidden. And Maya was using it for something far beyond what I could have imagined. Maybe it was linked to how she was controlling everything, watching Sarah, and keeping her secrets hidden. The pulse, the symbols—it was all part of something bigger.

But how could I figure out what it really did without waking her? I knew I had to try again, and this time, I would push further.

I hesitated, my hand hovering over Maya's wrist again, the strange pulse of the watch almost hypnotic in its steady rhythm. The flicker of the light made my heart race as I debated whether I should risk trying to activate it again. Every part of me screamed that I was dancing too close to danger, but I couldn't stop now. If this watch held the answers to everything Maya was hiding, I had to know.

I glanced around, making sure the others were still asleep. Eric and Theo's quiet breathing filled the cave, the soft crackle of the dying fire the only other sound. Maya shifted slightly in her sleep, her grip loosening on my hand, giving me the opportunity to slip my hand free.

This time, I steadied my breathing and leaned closer to the watch. The memory of those strange symbols flashing briefly before the screen went dark stuck in my mind. There had to be a pattern, a sequence, something to unlock it fully. My fingers hovered just above the watch face again, and I tried to remember the feeling when the glow intensified, the heat making it respond.

I exhaled softly, warming my fingertips again, letting the warmth radiate before I lowered my hand towards the watch. As my fingers neared the surface, the light flickered brighter once more, but this time, I traced my fingers along the air just above the surface, following an invisible pattern. It felt instinctual, like the symbols had burned into my mind, and as I followed that sensation, the watch seemed to respond.

Suddenly, a soft hum vibrated from the watch, and the face rippled again—this time more distinct. Symbols appeared, swirling in a circular formation like a code. I froze, watching as the surface changed, revealing a faint, holographic display just above it.

Numbers. Coordinates. Timers. My breath caught as I realized what I was seeing.

This wasn't just a watch.

It was some kind of tracking device.

There was a faint outline of a map, glowing faintly beneath the coordinates. And there, blinking on the map, were two points. One of them was right where we were—the cave. The other? My pulse quickened as I traced it further, to a remote location in the woods.

Was that where Tristan was? Could this be how Maya was watching people, controlling their movements? My mind raced with possibilities, but I couldn't linger too long. The coordinates shifted, and I saw a name flash across the screen—Sarah.

It was tracking her. That's how Maya knew everything. She was using this device to monitor Sarah's movements, keeping tabs on her every step.

I pulled my hand back, trying to steady my breathing. My heart pounded in my chest as the realization sank in. If Maya knew I had tampered with her watch, I'd be the next one she would track. My mind swirled with fear and the weight of what I'd uncovered.

I had to move fast, had to warn Sarah, had to figure out if Tristan was alive.

But as I leaned back, the watch gave one last pulse, and then went dark again, as if sensing that I was done. I exhaled slowly, slipping my hand away from Maya entirely. My head buzzed with everything I had learned, but I couldn't let on that I knew. Not yet.

I lay down, closing my eyes, pretending to sleep. But sleep wouldn't come. All I could see were those blinking coordinates and the unanswered question gnawing at me: Was Tristan out there somewhere, or was this another layer of Maya's twisted game?

PART 24 - THE CLOCKWORK LIE

As I lay there, pretending to sleep, my thoughts raced, swirling around the implications of what I had just discovered. Maya's watch wasn't just some device to keep time. It was a tool, a hidden way for her to control and monitor something or someone. Was this how she kept tabs on Sarah? How far did this connection go, and who else was involved?

Tristan.

That name echoed through my mind as I tried to make sense of everything. If the body in the cave wasn't him, then where was he? And if Maya had staged everything so perfectly, could it mean she was hiding him somewhere? Or worse—did she have him trapped, just like Sarah? The thought chilled me to the core.

Beside me, Maya's breathing was slow and steady, her hand still loosely wrapped around mine. I could feel the slight pulse in her fingers, a reminder of the calm she projected. But beneath that calm, I knew there was something darker at work. And now, with the watch, I had proof.

I waited for what felt like hours, listening to the others breathe, the occasional crackle of the fire dying down, and the distant rustle of the forest outside. The weight of the cave pressed down on me, but the tension in my chest was worse. I needed to act, but I couldn't rush it.

Finally, when I was sure Maya and the others were deeply asleep, I shifted slightly, glancing at the watch again. The faint glow was still there, barely visible under her wrist. My fingers itched to reach out, to figure out more, but I had to be careful. I couldn't let her know I was onto her.

No sudden movements, I told myself.

I took a deep breath, gathering the courage to try again. This time, I decided I needed to be more precise. I had to see what else that watch could reveal. Gently, I placed my hand over Maya's, feeling the cool metal against her skin. Slowly, I slid my thumb back to the side of the watch, where the display had appeared before.

Nothing at first. The screen remained blank, the same eerie silence surrounding me. But then, as I pressed just a bit harder, something clicked. A soft beep echoed in the quiet cave, and a hidden compartment on the side of the watch opened up. Inside was a tiny screen, displaying coordinates.

My breath caught.

Coordinates. Locations.

Was this how she tracked people? I scanned the numbers, but they didn't mean much to me in that moment. I'd need to memorize them—just in case. My mind worked quickly, trying to lock in the details before the screen went dark again.

But something else caught my attention—a small notification icon pulsed in the corner of the display. I carefully tapped it, and a message flashed across the screen:

Connection to Unit Active: 1 monitored. Status: Stable.1 monitored?

Was it Sarah? Was Maya tracking her every move, making sure she didn't try to escape again? My fingers hovered over the screen, trying to make sense of it all. Before I could go further, the screen blinked once, then twice, and abruptly went dark.

I pulled my hand away quickly, my pulse racing. The device had shut itself down, leaving no trace of the display. My heart pounded as I tried to process what I had just seen.

I turned my head slowly to look at Maya. She hadn't stirred, still lost in sleep, her breathing calm and rhythmic. But now, with everything I had uncovered, I saw her differently. This wasn't just about secrets. This was control—manipulation of a deeper kind.

I leaned back, careful not to make any sudden moves. My mind whirled with what I now knew. If Maya was tracking people, and manipulating events, then she was more dangerous than I had even realized.

As I lay there, sleep was impossible. I was trapped in this cave with Maya, Theo, and Eric, but now I didn't know who I could trust. Could Theo and Eric be part of this too? Or were they just as clueless as me? I needed to figure it out—and fast.

Morning couldn't come soon enough.

The rest of the night passed in tense silence. I didn't sleep. My mind wouldn't allow it, and my heart thudded anxiously in my chest. The weight of what I had uncovered felt like a stone pressing down on me. Every little sound in the cave, the shifting of someone's body, the crackling of dying embers, felt amplified in the quiet darkness.

I kept replaying Maya's words in my head: "I even planted his ring on that body in the cave. The cops won't question it."

If Tristan's body wasn't in the cave, where was he? Could he still be alive? And if so, why had Maya gone to such lengths to make everyone think he was dead? My mind churned with possibilities, none of them good.

Just as the first faint light of dawn filtered through the cave's entrance, Theo stirred, stretching and yawning quietly. I watched as he glanced at Maya and then at me, his face shadowed with exhaustion. He hadn't noticed anything out of the ordinary, but I couldn't help but feel a creeping suspicion toward him. What if he was in on it? What if Maya wasn't the only one pulling strings?

Theo rubbed his eyes and sat up, blinking blearily at me. "You okay?" he asked softly, his voice barely above a whisper.

I nodded, forcing a smile. "Yeah, just couldn't sleep."

He gave a small grunt of understanding before glancing toward Maya, who was still sleeping soundly. "She didn't wake up all night," he murmured, his gaze shifting back to me. "That's rare for her."

I swallowed, unsure of how to respond. The watch flashed in my mind again. I hadn't even told Theo or Eric what I had discovered. I wasn't ready. Not yet. I had to figure out who I could trust first.

Eric woke soon after, rubbing his arms as if trying to shake off the stiffness of sleeping on the cold cave floor. "Let's pack up and get moving," he muttered, his tone weary. "We can't stay here forever."

Maya stirred at the sound of his voice, stretching and yawning in a way that seemed almost too relaxed for someone who had so much to hide. Her eyes flicked over to me, and for a moment, I thought I saw a flicker of something in her gaze—something calculating. But just as quickly, she smiled, her expression softening.

"Did you sleep at all?" she asked, her voice gentle as she moved closer to me, her hand reaching out as if she genuinely cared.

I stiffened as her fingers brushed mine again, and I fought the urge to pull away. "Not much," I muttered, trying to keep my tone casual. "Just... a lot on my mind."

Her grip on my hand tightened ever so slightly, and she leaned in closer, her voice low. "We'll figure it out," she whispered, her breath warm against my ear. "Together."

There was an unsettling edge to her words. I nodded, not trusting myself to speak. The last thing I needed was for her to suspect that I knew more than I let on.

As we packed up, I found myself glancing at Maya's wrist again. The watch was still there, innocuous in the daylight, just a simple accessory. But I knew better now. I had to find out more about it. It was the key to unlocking whatever was going on with her, and possibly with Tristan.As we made our way out of the cave, I walked behind Maya, watching her closely. Every time she raised her wrist, every time the sunlight glinted off the face of the watch, I felt a surge of tension in my gut. She had more control over this situation than any of us realized.

Theo led the way, his eyes scanning the trees ahead. Eric followed close behind, his shoulders tense. Neither of them had any idea what was really happening. They didn't know the darkness that lingered just beneath the surface of our group.

Hours passed as we trekked through the forest, the silence heavy between us. I couldn't stop thinking about what Maya had said to Sarah, about the people she had watching Sarah. How was she keeping tabs on her? Was it all connected to that watch?

We stopped by a creek to rest, and as the others bent down to fill their water bottles, I saw my chance. Maya was distracted, talking to Eric about the route we'd take next. I slipped behind her, my eyes on the watch again.

It was now or never.

With my hand trembling slightly, I reached out and tapped the side of the watch, hoping to activate it like I had last night. At first, nothing happened, but I didn't give up. I tried again, this time sliding my fingers across the face of the watch in a slow, deliberate motion.

There it was. The faint glow reappeared, flickering to life. My heart pounded as the screen blinked on, revealing the same coordinates from before. But this time, there was something else—a new notification flashing across the screen:

Connection to Unit Active: 2 monitored. Status: Pending.

Two monitored. My blood ran cold. Another person? Who was the second?

I tried to tap the notification for more information, but suddenly, Maya's voice broke through the quiet. "Hey, what are you doing?"

I jerked my hand back, the screen instantly going dark. I turned to see Maya watching me, her eyes narrowing slightly, suspicion creeping into her expression.

My mind raced for an excuse. "I thought you had a cool watch," I said, trying to sound casual. "Just checking it out."

She smiled, but there was a hint of something cold behind her eyes. "It's just a watch," she said smoothly. "Nothing special."

I nodded, forcing a laugh. "Yeah, just curious."

Maya turned away, but I could feel her watching me from the corner of her eye. She knew something was up. I had to be more careful. One wrong move, and she would figure out that I was onto her.

As we started walking again, my mind raced. Two people. She was monitoring two people. Could the second person be Tristan? Was he still alive, hidden somewhere in the depths of these woods? Or worse—was he close by, trapped in a place we hadn't yet discovered?

The possibilities churned in my mind, but one thing was certain: I had to find out. And I had to do it before Maya realized just how much I knew.

PART 25 - TANGLED LOYALTIES

As we trudged through the dense forest, the events of the previous night still echoed in my mind. The air was thick with the scent of damp earth and pine needles, a stark contrast to the chaos that had just unfolded. We moved in a daze, our hearts heavy with the memories of fear and uncertainty. Just when I thought I might drown in those memories, a sudden thundering sound shattered the stillness around us.

I looked up, and there it was—a helicopter slicing through the sky like a silver bullet. My heart raced as realization dawned. We weren't alone anymore. Relief surged through me, pulling me from the depths of despair, and I couldn't help but shout and wave my arms frantically. "Over here! We're here!" My voice broke through the trees, a desperate call for salvation.

The helicopter descended toward us, its blades whirring like a wild beast awakened. As it landed, a whirlwind of leaves and dust spiraled around us, transforming the clearing into a storm of nature. The moment the doors swung open, our fathers emerged, their faces a mix of relief and anxiety. I could barely process their expressions before they were rushing toward us, their voices cutting through the chaos.

"Maya! Theo!" her dad shouted, panic evident in his tone. "What were you thinking, going out here without telling us?"

Theo's dad joined in, his eyes wide with concern as he scanned us for any signs of harm. "We were worried sick! Do you have any idea how dangerous it is out here?"

Tristan's dad staggered forward, his voice trembling with emotion. "I can't lose you all like I lost my son. You're like my children." He enveloped us in a desperate embrace, his arms wrapping around us as if he could shield himself from the haunting memory of his lost boy. The warmth of his body was a stark reminder of what we had almost lost, and I found myself squeezing him tightly, fighting back tears.

Once aboard the helicopter, the atmosphere shifted. The relief of being found mingled with an unspoken tension that hung in the air. We were all silent, processing the gravity of our ordeal. Maya sat next to me, her hands trembling in her lap. She stared out the window, her expression unreadable as the trees shrank beneath us, giving way to a vast expanse of green that felt both liberating and suffocating. I couldn't shake the feeling that something was off about her, a tension that seemed to radiate from her.

After what felt like hours of silence, we finally landed back in town. The sight of the familiar landscape was both comforting and disconcerting. It felt like stepping back into a life that had been irreparably altered. As we stepped off the helicopter, the chaos of the world rushed back in, with reporters and police officers swarming around us, their questions flying like arrows.

"Maya! What happened in the woods?" one reporter yelled, his camera flashing.

"Did you see Tristan?" another called, desperation creeping into her voice.

The weight of their questions pressed down on me, and I found it hard to breathe. We were immediately ushered away from the throng, led into a small conference room where the police waited, their expressions grave.

"Alright, we need to talk," one officer said, his voice steady but firm. "We have a lot of questions about what happened during your time in the woods."

The questioning began, and I recounted our harrowing experience in the cave, my voice trembling as I spoke. "We saw something bad," I told them, struggling to keep my composure. "But I don't know if it was him—we didn't see the face."

Maya's voice cut through the stillness, unwavering and sharp. "I'm certain it was Tristan's ring. It had to be him." Her words hung in the air, heavy and ominous.

Theo and Eric nodded in agreement, their faces pale as they tried to piece together the fragmented story. "Yeah, we didn't see the face clearly, but it felt like it could be him," Theo added, his voice barely above a whisper, laced with fear.

I hesitated, a storm of uncertainty raging within me, but eventually nodded along, though doubt gnawed at my insides. "It might be him," I murmured, but the insistent whisper in my mind warned me of the shadows lurking in the truth.

Once the questioning ended, we were dismissed, but the weight of our experience lingered in the air like a storm cloud. Days turned into a tense silence; we didn't talk much, each of us lost in our own thoughts, struggling with the consequences of the nightmare we had endured.

It was only two days later when I found the courage to call Eric and Theo. "Can you both meet me?" I urged, my heart racing with urgency. "And don't tell Maya."

"Why would you say that?" Eric asked.

"I said it like that because I felt something was off with Maya," I replied.

I wasted no time. I filled them in on everything I had discovered about Maya and the watch, the secrets I had unearthed while they were asleep. Their expressions shifted from confusion to shock as I recounted the details of that fateful night.

"Heat-sensitive watch ?" Eric asked disbelief etched on his face.

"It's not just any watch," I explained, my heart pounding in my chest. "It has a hidden compartment, and it showed coordinates. I think Maya was using it to keep tabs on Sarah and maybe Tristan."

Eric shook his head, the hurt evident in his eyes. "My sister wouldn't do something like that! There must be a reason, a misunderstanding."

"Maya was acting strange," I insisted, feeling the urgency of the moment. "And she was so sure it was Tristan's body. We need to figure this out together."

Theo nodded, determination etching his features. "We can't just sit back and let this go. If Maya's involved in something shady, we have to get to the bottom of it."

The three of us huddled together, a makeshift team forged in the fires of uncertainty. We were fueled by a mix of fear and resolve, knowing we had to uncover the truth about Maya, the watch, and the mystery of Tristan's disappearance. But as we embarked on this dangerous path, I couldn't shake the feeling that the shadows were closing in, hiding secrets we weren't yet prepared to confront.

As we began to devise a plan, Eric's expression darkened. "What if Maya is in over her head? What if she's caught up in something dangerous?" His words echoed in the silence, a reminder of the risks we were facing.

The more we talked, the more the weight of our situation sank in. Maya had always been the one we relied on, A friend, A sister, who brought us together. But now, with the looming suspicion that she might be hiding something, it felt as if the ground was shifting beneath us. Each revelation about the watch deepened the chasm between us and her.

The next day was filled with restless energy as we tried to gather information, scouring the internet for any news regarding Tristan and the police investigation. We found reports of the body that had been discovered, but there were inconsistencies in the details. "They said it was mauled by an animal, but what if..." Theo hesitated, glancing at Eric and me. "What if they're wrong? What if that body isn't even Tristan?"

I felt a chill run down my spine. "What if Maya knew about it? What if she did something to protect herself or hide the truth?"

The three of us exchanged glances, the tension palpable.

We had to confront Maya, but how could we do that without risking everything we had left? The friendship we shared felt fragile, a thin thread hanging in the balance. Eric, especially, seemed torn, grappling with the possibility that his sister was involved in something sinister.

"I can't believe this is happening," Eric said, his voice barely a whisper. "I don't want to think about my sister like this."

I reached out, placing a hand on his shoulder. "We'll figure this out together, Eric. We won't let her drag us down with her if she's hiding something."

After a long pause, Theo spoke up. "What if we confront her together? Maybe we can get her to reveal what she knows about the watch and the body."

Eric hesitated, his brow furrowing. "I don't want to put her on the defensive. She might just shut down. I know her. If she feels cornered..."

"But we can't let this go on," I insisted. "We need answers."

Part 26 - Confronting Shadows

The air felt electric with anticipation as we gathered in Theo's dimly lit garage, the only light coming from a single bulb hanging overhead.

The atmosphere was thick with unsaid words, each of us aware that we were on the precipice of something monumental. Eric paced back and forth, his hands shoved deep into his pockets, while Theo and I exchanged nervous glances.

"We can't keep dancing around this," I said, breaking the silence. "We need to know what Maya knows." Eric stopped pacing, running a hand through his hair.

"Let's keep it casual," Theo suggested, leaning against the workbench. "We can invite her for ice cream or something. A safe space where she won't feel attacked.

"Eric nodded slowly, his expression still troubled. "That could work, but we have to be careful with our questions."

We decided to text Maya, suggesting we meet at our favorite ice cream shop, a cozy place that felt like a second home. The three of us waited anxiously, each of us lost in our thoughts as we checked our phones repeatedly, half-hoping for a quick reply.

It felt like we were gearing up for a storm, unsure of what the clouds would bring.When Maya finally responded, her message was brief: "Sure, I'll be there in a bit."

My stomach knotted with a mix of relief and apprehension. As we arrived at the shop, the familiar scent of waffle cones and freshly churned ice cream filled the air, but it did little to ease my anxiety. We chose a booth in the back corner, away from prying eyes, and fidgeted with our menus, trying to keep the mood light as we waited for Maya to arrive.

She walked in just a few minutes later, her expression brightening when she spotted us.

"Hey, guys!" she called, waving as she approached. But as she sat down, I noticed the slight hesitation in her smile, the way her eyes darted around the shop before settling on us. Something felt off, and the tension in the air tightened around us like a noose.

The air was heavy with the sweet scent of waffle cones and melting chocolate as we settled into a booth at the ice cream shop. The clatter of spoons against bowls and the laughter of families filled the space, creating a bizarre contrast to the weight hanging over us. Maya sat across from Eric and me, her gaze fixed on the colorful array of flavors behind the counter.

"Thanks for coming, Maya," I said, trying to keep my voice steady. Eric was fidgeting, his fingers tapping against the table, the tension radiating between us palpable.

"Yeah, I mean, I guess I was wondering why you wanted to meet here," she replied, her voice laced with uncertainty.

"We just wanted to talk about everything," Eric said, leaning forward, his expression earnest.

"About what happened in the woods. We need to understand what we saw."

Maya shifted in her seat, her expression guarded. "I already told you guys everything. It was dark; I don't know what we saw."

"But you were so sure it was Tristan," I pressed, feeling the need to break through the wall she had built around herself. "Why? What made you so certain?"

Her eyes darted away, and for a moment, I caught a glimpse of something raw—fear, regret, perhaps even guilt. "It was the ring," she murmured, her voice barely above a whisper.

Eric's brow furrowed. "But we didn't see his face. How can you be sure?"

Maya hesitated, biting her lip. "I just know," she said, her tone defiant yet tinged with uncertainty. "It had to be him."

I exchanged a glance with Eric, and the air in the booth felt heavier. "Maya, what if we told you we think Tristan isn't dead?" I asked cautiously.

Her gaze sharpened, and for the first time, I saw a flicker of something darker behind her eyes. "You think he's alive?"

"Maybe," I replied, testing the waters. "But we need to know what happened that night. If there's more to the story, you need to tell us."

She leaned back, crossing her arms, her expression hardening. "You want to know what happened? Fine. Tristan isn't dead. He's with Sarah."

"Sarah?" I echoed, bewildered. "His girlfriend?"

Maya's lips curled into a smirk that sent a chill down my spine. "You think you know the story, but you don't. Sarah and

I—we've got plans. Tristan is in a cabin under the waterfalls, and he's not alone. He's part of something bigger now, something you can't even begin to understand."

Eric looked between us, confusion etched on his face. "What are you talking about?"

Maya's eyes gleamed with a dangerous intensity. "You thought you were the hero of this story, didn't you? But you're not. I'm not a crybaby. I'm not weak. I have an army, and Tristan will be mine again. You should have known better than to think you could just waltz in and take him away from me."

The weight of her words hung in the air like a dark cloud, and my heart raced as realization settled in. Maya was no longer the innocent friend caught in a web of confusion; she was the villain in our story.

"You think I'm scared of you?" I challenged, trying to regain control of the conversation. "You think we won't do anything to find Tristan?"

Maya leaned in, her smile now unsettling. "You'll regret underestimating me. I won't let anyone take him from me again."

With that, she stood up, tossing a few bills onto the table. "Enjoy your ice cream. You'll need it while you can still taste freedom."

As she walked out of the shop, the weight of her revelation crushed down on us. Eric and I sat in stunned silence, the colorful world of ice cream and laughter around us feeling like a cruel joke.

"She can't be serious," Eric finally said, disbelief etched on his face.

I shook my head, my mind racing. "We have to find Tristan before it's too late."

In that moment, we understood that the stakes had risen. This was no longer just about the mystery of Tristan's disappearance; it was a battle against someone who would stop at nothing to claim him for herself.

Maya's revelation hung heavy in the air as we processed what she had said about her plans with Sarah.

Eric and I exchanged glances, the unease twisting deeper within us. The weight of her words sank in, but I couldn't shake the feeling that something far more sinister was at play.

I recalled a moment earlier that night at the cave when she slipped away, mentioning she wanted to go to the toilet. I had followed her, my instincts screaming that something was off.

"I followed her," I said, my voice low as I pulled Eric and Theo closer, ensuring our conversation stayed private amidst the chaos of the shop. "I thought it was just a bathroom break, but she disappeared into the shadows."

"What do you mean?" Theo asked, brow furrowing in confusion.

"She went under the ground," I explained, my heart racing as I recalled the memory. "I followed her into the back alley, and that's when I saw her. She had Sarah tied up, and I think Tristan is in another cabin."

Eric's eyes widened. "What? You're saying she's got them both?"

"I'm saying there were two coordinates on the watch," I replied, trying to keep my voice steady.

"One was for where Sarah is, and the other... it has to be where Tristan is. But why would she trap Sarah?"

Theo leaned forward, intrigued. "But how do you know it's Tristan? What if it's someone else?"

"Because I hoped so," I admitted the truth weighing heavily on my chest. "This isn't just about finding out if he's trapped or got killed,

It's about uncovering what Maya's army is planning, what they're actually doing. She's not just some friend—she's orchestrating something."

The realization settled in, heavy and unsettling. Maya had formed a network, a force of her own, and it was clear she intended to use it to her advantage.

"What if she's trying to manipulate Tristan?" Theo pondered, his expression thoughtful. "If she's using Sarah to get to him, what does that mean for us?"

Eric shook his head, frustration bubbling to the surface. "We need to figure out what her endgame is. If she's got an army, then she's serious about whatever plan she's hatching."

I felt a rush of urgency. "We can't wait any longer. We have to find out where they are—both Sarah and Tristan. If Maya is capable of this, who knows what else she's willing to do?"

Theo's face hardened with determination. "We need to split up, gather information. If we can find out more about Maya's army, maybe we can outsmart her."

As we formulated a plan, my mind raced with images of what Maya was capable of. She was no longer the girl I had grown up with; she had transformed into a formidable force, and I couldn't help but wonder how deep her betrayal ran.

"We should start with the cabin by the waterfalls," I suggested, my pulse quickening at the thought of confronting Maya.

"It's close enough that we can investigate without being detected. But we need to be careful."

As we finalized our plan, a heavy sense of dread settled over me. The world around us seemed to pulse with danger, and I couldn't shake the feeling that time was slipping away.

Maya was playing a dangerous game, and we were running out of time to uncover the truth.

The next steps were clear: we would find Sarah, discover the location of Tristan, and unveil Maya's hidden agenda before it was too late. As we prepared to move out, the weight of our mission loomed large, and I steeled myself for the confrontation ahead.

PART 27 - VANISHED IN THIN AIR

As we gathered our thoughts in the booth, the memories of that night in the woods came rushing back. I closed my eyes, trying to piece together the fragments of our experience.

"Remember when we stumbled upon that house?" I asked, my voice tinged with urgency. "That's where we found Tristan's picture."

Theo nodded slowly. "Yeah, it was strange. I think Maya was the one who found it first, right?"

"Exactly," I replied, feeling the weight of realization settle in.

"She led us there, didn't she? Who else would know that house was even there?"

Eric's brow furrowed in contemplation. "She sighed and suggested we go that way. It's all starting to connect."

"Do you see it now, Eric?" I pressed, leaning forward. "This was all part of Maya's plan. Everything was a scam! She wanted us to get trapped while we thought we were trying to find Tristan."

Theo looked uneasy, his expression shifting from confusion to understanding. "So she set this up to keep us distracted while she worked on whatever scheme she has going on."

Eric rubbed his temples, frustration etched across his face. "This isn't just about finding Tristan anymore. It's about Maya manipulating us the whole time."

"We can't go alone, not after everything that's happened," Theo said firmly. "We need to involve the cops."

"Yes, we'll take them with us," Eric agreed, determination igniting in his eyes. "We can't let her pull us into another trap. We need backup, and we need to get to the bottom of this."

I felt a surge of adrenaline at the thought of confronting Maya. The sense of betrayal burned deep, but it also fueled my resolve.

"If she's hiding something, we'll find it. We'll expose her plans and rescue Sarah and Tristan if they're still alive."

Theo nodded, his face set with determination. "We'll have to act quickly. The longer we wait, the more chances Maya has to cover her tracks."

"Let's gather everything we know and go to the police," Eric said, standing up with renewed vigor. "We'll present our findings and make sure they take us seriously."

As we moved to leave the ice cream shop, I couldn't shake the feeling of dread that hung over us. Maya had become a puppet master, and we were just players in her game. But I wasn't about to let her win.

We stepped out into the cool evening air, our minds racing with plans and possibilities. The shadows loomed around us, but I felt a flicker of hope igniting within. We were determined to uncover the truth, no matter the cost.

The next day dawned with an unsettling chill in the air, an omen of the journey we were about to undertake. After a restless night filled with doubts, we gathered our courage and met outside the woods. Officer Harris had agreed to join us, along with a couple of other officers, but I felt a heavy weight on my chest as we approached the spot Maya had led us to before.

"Are you sure this is the right place?" Officer Harris asked, scanning the area.

"This is where she went in," I said my voice barely above a whisper.

As we walked, each step felt heavier than the last, like the earth itself was warning us to turn back. The trees loomed above us, casting shadows that danced eerily in the sunlight. My heart raced as we reached the hidden entrance to the underground vent—a rusty, old hatch half-covered by foliage.

"Here it is," I said, lifting the hatch with trembling hands. The cold air wafted up from below, sending shivers down my spine.

"Everyone stay close," Officer Harris instructed, leading the way into the dark.

The descent was steep, with each creaking step echoing around us. A cold chill enveloped us, making it feel as if the very walls were alive, whispering secrets of the past. I glanced back at Eric, Theo, and the officers, their faces a mixture of apprehension and determination.

The further we went down, the more the atmosphere shifted; the air thickened with tension and dread. I led them to the last turn, my heart racing with anticipation of what we might find. But as we reached the end of the staircase, I was met with an unsettling emptiness.

"Where is the cabin?" Eric whispered, glancing around, confusion etched on his face.

"It should be right here!" I said, panic rising in my chest. "This is where I saw Maya and Sarah that night!"

I rushed forward, searching for any signs, any remnants of what might have been, but the space was barren. No cabin. No furniture. Nothing but cold, damp walls and the echo of our breaths. It was as if Maya had anticipated our investigation and stripped everything away, leaving no trace behind.

"The place is empty," Officer Harris muttered, his voice laced with frustration. "This doesn't make sense."

"That's exactly it," I said, piecing it all together in my mind. "Maya knew we would come back. She wanted us to find this place, but she's taken everything. She's powerful enough to orchestrate all of this without leaving a single clue behind."

As I spoke, a shiver crawled down my spine. "We're just pawns in her game."

"What do we do now?" Theo asked, desperation creeping into his voice.

"First, we need to get out of here," Officer Harris replied, his tone authoritative. "We'll regroup and figure out our next steps."

But just as we turned to leave, I felt a strange sense of foreboding. What if Maya was watching us? What if she had planned for us to come here, only to lead us into a trap?

As we made our way back up the stairs, the weight of our failure pressed down on me. We had entered a world where nothing was as it seemed, and the chilling realization hit me: Maya wasn't just a friend caught in a web of deception; she was the spider, and we were the flies.

Once outside, I took a deep breath, the sunlight striking my face, warming my chilled skin. But that warmth was quickly overshadowed by the looming shadow of uncertainty. We were running out of time, and I feared that Maya's grip on the situation was tightening.

"We need to keep searching," I urged. "We can't let her get away with this."

Eric nodded, his expression resolute. "We'll find a way to expose her. We have to."

With Officer Harris's support, we made a plan to investigate further, determined to uncover the truth. Maya had cleared the evidence, but I felt in my gut that the deeper we dug, the more we would discover about her sinister game. And somewhere beneath it all, I hoped to find Tristan before it was too late.

PART 28 - UNEXPECTED CONFESSION

When we arrived back at the station, Officer Harris shifted in his chair, skepticism shadowing his features. "You kids need to be careful with accusations. Without concrete evidence, it's just hearsay," he warned, his voice tinged with impatience.

"Sorry," I said, feeling the weight of our desperation hang in the air. "But we really think Maya is involved in something serious."

"Take your time," he replied, "but be careful. These things can escalate quickly."

As we exited, the tension was palpable. Theo furrowed his brow, deep in thought. "Why would Maya say, 'I won't let anyone take him from me again?'"

Eric shrugged, his eyes distant. "It doesn't make sense. She's hiding something."

"Why did you say, 'Do not enter your room' at the resort that day?" I pressed Eric, my curiosity piqued.

"Let's get out of here," he said, dragging me and Theo toward a nearby café. Once inside, he leaned closer, lowering his voice. "Daisy, I love you."

Theo's eyes widened in shock. "I saw that coming," he murmured, glancing between us.

"This isn't the right time," I replied, trying to keep the situation from spiraling.

"I know we're supposed to be focused on finding Tristan, even if he's alive. Do you think he would love you when we find him?" Asked Eric.

"Of course not," Theo interjected, his tone serious. "He has Sarah, right?"

"Exactly," Eric agreed, his expression earnest. "You need to forget Tristan. That day I was about to surprise you, and I still want to show you."

Before I could respond, Eric opened the café door, ushering me into the front seat of his car.

Theo climbed in the back seat, his expression a mix of concern and curiosity.

"Where are we going?" I asked, feeling the adrenaline from earlier still pulsing through me.

"To the resort," Eric said, a playful glint in his eye. "The room upstairs."

Once we arrived, I followed Eric's lead as he guided us up the stairs. He paused outside a door, a mischievous smile on his face. "Open that door, Daisy," he instructed, his voice steady but excited.

Tension knotted in my stomach as I reached for the handle, my heart racing. When I opened the door, I was greeted by a breathtaking sight. Balloons floated in a kaleidoscope of colors, each one glimmering softly in the warm light.

Pictures of me hung from the walls, captured moments from when I was about eleven years old, all adorned with delicate ribbons that cascaded from the ceiling. My childhood laughter echoed in my mind, intertwining with the warmth of the memories.

But the most striking was a poem Eric had written on the wall behind the bed. Each line spoke to the depths of my heart, words that seemed to dance off the page and wrap around me like a comforting embrace.

I stood there, overwhelmed. "I can't believe this," I whispered, tears of gratitude pooling in my eyes. I turned to Eric, my voice trembling with emotion. "Thankyou"

Theo, still processing, leaned against the wall, watching us with a knowing smile. "Don't think anything, Daisy. Just say yes," he urged gently.

Eric stepped closer, his expression softening. "I may just be a chapter in your story, but you are my entire novel. Can I be all the chapters in your life's tale?"

My heart swelled with the weight of his words. "Yes," I breathed, the word spilling from my lips like a long-awaited release.

The air felt charged with possibilities, a moment suspended in time, as I embraced the unexpected love that had blossomed amidst the chaos surrounding us.As I stepped back from Eric, my heart still fluttering with the weight of his words, I caught Theo's eye. His expression was a complex mix of surprise and something else—perhaps a touch of sadness. I could tell he was grappling with the reality of our situation.

"I'm happy for you both," he added, though his smile didn't quite reach his eyes. "Really, I am." It was a valiant effort to mask the twist of emotions within him.

Eric, sensing the delicate atmosphere, turned to Theo. "Thanks, man. I know this might be... complicated."

Theo nodded, his gaze drifting momentarily before locking onto mine. "Just make sure you take care of her, Eric. Daisy deserves that."

I appreciated the sentiment, even if it stung a little, knowing it stemmed from a place of past connection. "I will," Eric promised, his voice earnest.

Theo took a deep breath, shaking off whatever had clouded his thoughts. "You know, it's good to see you both happy. I just hope... I hope things stay simple for you. With everything going on..."

As he trailed off, I could see the shadow of concern creeping back into his eyes. I stepped forward, reaching out to place a reassuring hand on his shoulder. "We'll figure it all out, Theo. I promise."

"Yeah, it's just," he started, looking a little lost. "With everything that happened with Tristan, I don't want any of us to get hurt again."

The weight of his words hung heavy in the air, a reminder of the chaos that had brought us here. I nodded, appreciating his protectiveness, even as I felt the bittersweet tug of our past. With a final shared look, I knew this moment—this new chapter—would come with its own set of challenges, but for now, I felt a surge of hope, ready to embrace whatever lay ahead.

As the moment between us lingered, Eric reached into his backpack, pulling out my artsy diary. His smile was warm and genuine, and as he handed it to me, his eyes sparkled with a hint of mischief.

"Here, I thought you might want to capture this moment," he said, his voice softening. "Write down today's date. It's special."

I felt a flutter in my chest as I took the diary, tracing my fingers over the worn cover. It had been my companion through so many emotions, and now it would hold yet another beautiful memory. I opened it to a fresh page, the crisp paper waiting to be filled with my thoughts.

As I wrote the date, I glanced up at Eric, whose gaze was fixed on me with an intensity that made my heart race. "What should I write?" I asked, grinning.

He shrugged, leaning back against the wall, looking utterly content. "Just be honest. Write from the heart."

I took a deep breath, letting inspiration wash over me, and began to write:"From the gentle nudge to step into their world,To finding comfort in the space they create for me,From making sense of the unsaid, To being understood before the words even come, From taking invaluable presents, To treasuring the moments of life— I have achieved the love of my life"As I finished, I smiled at my creation, feeling the words resonate with the feelings swirling around us. Eric leaned over, reading my poem, his smile widening with each line."I love it," he said softly, admiration shining in his eyes. "You have a way with words, Daisy. It's beautiful."

"Thanks," I replied, warmth flooding my cheeks. "It's just how I feel."

He shifted closer, his shoulder brushing against mine as he glanced at the diary again. "You know, I hope we can create many more moments worth writing about."

I nodded, my heart racing at the thought. "We will, Eric. This is just the beginning."

He grinned, and in that moment, everything felt right. The world outside faded away, leaving just the two of us in our own little bubble of happiness. It was as if time had paused, allowing us to savor the beauty of now.

Part 29 - Tangled

As the warm glow of our newfound happiness enveloped us, my phone buzzed in my pocket, pulling me back to reality. I glanced at Theo, who had an intense look on his face as he answered the call.

"Hello? Officer Harris?" he said, his tone shifting from relaxed to alert.

I felt my heart race as I leaned in closer, straining to catch every word.

"Yeah, I understand. We'll be right there." He hung up and turned to us, urgency etched on his features.

"They've found Maya. Her coordinates connected with the local network, but they couldn't locate Tristan or Sarah."

The air shifted around us, heavy with tension. Eric's expression hardened, determination flickering in his eyes.

"We need to go. Now." Without hesitation, we rushed to Eric's car, the excitement of the earlier moments now replaced with a frantic energy.

As we sped through the winding roads, the weight of our mission settled on our shoulders like a heavy cloak.

"What do you think Maya is planning?" I asked, my voice barely above a whisper, the shadows of uncertainty creeping back in.

"I don't know, but we can't let her slip away again," Theo replied, glancing out the window as the trees blurred past us. Eric's knuckles turned white as he gripped the steering wheel.

"We'll get answers, and this time, we won't be distracted by anything else." Arriving at the location where Maya was found, we stepped out of the car, our hearts pounding with a mix of fear and resolve. The air felt charged, a storm brewing inside each of us as we approached the police perimeter.

Officer Harris stood at the edge, his brow furrowed in concern. "They've got her in custody, but we still need to search the area for Tristan and Sarah. You kids should wait here."

"No way," Eric interjected, shaking his head. "We're not leaving until we know what's going on."

"Yeah," I added, feeling a surge of adrenaline. "Maya might know where they are."Theo nodded, his eyes set on the scene before us.

"We need to stick together. Whatever happens next, we face it as a team."

As the officers began their search, we hovered nearby, a nervous energy pulsating between us. We exchanged glances, silently acknowledging the stakes of this confrontation. Maya was dangerous, and if she had been orchestrating everything behind the scenes, we were standing on the brink of something much larger than ourselves.

Moments later, the police vehicle pulled up, and a few officers emerged, leading Maya away. Her expression was a mixture of defiance and satisfaction, and as her gaze met mine, a shiver ran down my spine.

"Hey, Daisy!" she called out, a smirk playing on her lips. "Did you really think you could find Tristan without me? You're all just pawns in this game."

The officers tightened their grip on her, leading her toward the station. Eric stepped forward, anger flickering in his eyes.

"What have you done with them, Maya?"

Her laugh echoed in the silence, chilling me to the bone.

"You'll find out soon enough. But don't worry; I've made sure they're safe... for now."

With those words, she was taken away, leaving us in a whirlwind of uncertainty.

As we regrouped, I could feel the weight of the mystery pressing down on us.

We had to dig deeper, find out what Maya was truly capable of, and uncover the truth behind her web of lies.

"Let's not waste any time," Theo urged. "We need to find clues. There has to be something she left behind."

With renewed determination, we set out to search the area, fueled by the urgency of the moment and the hope that we could uncover the truth about Tristan and Sarah before it was too late.

As the sun dipped lower in the sky, casting long shadows over the scene, the urgency of our mission intensified.

Eric, Theo, and I began combing through the area where Maya had been found, our minds racing with the implications of her words.

"Why would Maya trap Sarah and Tristan?" I murmured, more to myself than to the others.

"What could she possibly gain?"Theo knelt beside a tangle of brush, inspecting something on the ground.

"There's got to be a reason," he said, his voice steady despite the uncertainty.

"Maya isn't just playing games; she's always been strategic. This isn't just about revenge; it's personal."

Eric stood nearby, his expression thoughtful.

"Maya and Sarah have been friends for a long time. What if this is about jealousy? What if she's envious of the life they've built together?"

My heart raced as an idea began to take shape. "But that wouldn't explain why she'd go after Tristan. She's always acted like a loyal friend. What if this goes deeper? What if it's not just about jealousy, but about control?"

Theo stood up, brushing dirt from his hands.

"Control? You mean she wants to be the one in charge of their destinies, like she feels she lost control in her own life?"

"Exactly," I replied, a flicker of understanding igniting my thoughts.

"She's been acting like the puppet master. If she sees herself as powerful, this could be her way of asserting that power over the one person who seemingly has it all—Tristan."

Eric's face paled as the realization hit him. "And if she feels abandoned by him, maybe she believes that trapping them will bring them back under her influence, even if it's twisted. She wants them to see that they need her."

"Like she wants to show them that they can't escape her," I added, a sense of dread settling in my stomach. "This is about

Maya needing validation. She's trying to prove she can hold their lives in her hands."

Suddenly, Theo's voice broke through the tension. "Look! Over here!" He gestured to a patch of dirt where something glimmered. We rushed over to find an ornate locket half-buried, its surface scratched but still beautiful. I picked it up, dusting it off to reveal intricate engravings on the front. As I opened it, I found two pictures—one of Maya and Tristan, and another of Sarah, smiling brightly.

"What is this doing here?" Eric asked, eyeing the locket warily."It's a piece of her past," I said slowly, realizing the significance.

"This must have meant something to her. Maybe she's using it as leverage. To keep them in line."

"That makes sense," Theo said, his mind racing.

"If she wants them to feel guilty or indebted to her, she'd hold onto memories like this to control their emotions."

Suddenly, the pieces began to fall into place. "What if she's trying to recreate the bond they once had? Maybe she believes that by manipulating their feelings, she can regain the affection they once shared," I suggested, my voice gaining strength.

"She's trying to rewrite their history so that they'll realize they can't move forward without her." Eric frowned, running a hand through his hair.

"But that's a dangerous game. She's risking everything. If they escape, her plan collapses."

As we absorbed this revelation, a sense of urgency surged within us. We needed to find Tristan and Sarah before Maya could execute her plan fully. "Let's head to the area where Maya was caught," I said, resolute.

"If she has been leaving clues or messages, that's where we'll find them. We can't let her keep them under her thumb any longer."

With our minds focused on the next steps, we quickly made our way back to Officer Harris,

"We need your help," Theo said, urgency lacing his voice. "Maya's got a bigger plan. She's trying to manipulate their feelings. If we don't act fast, she could hurt them."

Harris raised an eyebrow, skepticism creeping back into his expression. "And how do you know this?"

I held up the locket, its weight suddenly feeling heavy in my hand. "This was found near where Maya was apprehended. It shows her connection to them, and her intent to control them through emotional manipulation."

He studied the locket for a moment, then looked back at us, the lines on his forehead easing slightly. "All right, if you truly believe this, we can't waste time. Let's get a team together and head out."

As we gathered our thoughts, I could feel the energy shift. We were no longer just searching for Tristan and Sarah; we were stepping into a battle against Maya's twisted grasp on their lives. With every step we took, the stakes grew higher, but we were ready to face whatever lay ahead.

As the reality of Maya's plan unraveled, Officer Harris led her into the interrogation room. Eric, his face pale and tense, was holding back a whirlwind of emotions. This wasn't the Maya he thought he knew; this was someone else entirely, someone darkened by jealousy and betrayal. The officers closed the door behind her, and in the dimly lit room, Maya sat, restrained but still defiant.

In the silence, Sarah's parents' anguished voices echoed down the hall as they demanded answers, their grief raw and searing. The weight of the situation bore down on everyone present, suffocating, thick with a mix of disbelief and anger. Eric stepped forward, the conflict in his eyes painful to witness.

"Maya," he began, his voice breaking. "Why did you do this? Why would you put Sarah and Tristan through something so terrible?"

Maya's gaze flickered over him, her calm cracking, just slightly. Her mouth opened, then closed, but something in Eric's face made her pause. She took a shaky breath, her defiance slipping, and when she finally spoke, her voice was low and filled with a dangerous calm.

"I wanted things to stay the same, Eric," she whispered. "Tristan and I...we were supposed to be together, friends forever. But then Daisy came along, and even though I tolerated her, Sarah changed everything." Her gaze hardened. "Sarah had no right to come between us, to push me away from him."

My stomach twisted as I realized where this was going. I had been part of the story, a chapter, but Sarah had become a defining line for Maya—a boundary Maya couldn't accept.

Maya's voice wavered, then sharpened. "When Sarah told Tristan not to speak to me, it was like she was pulling the rug out from under me. I tried to hold back. I swallowed it all. But that night at the bar, when I was drunk, I let it all out. I kissed him, told him how I felt."

Eric's face fell, and he looked away as if seeing something he could never unsee.

"He rejected me," Maya continued, a bitter smile tugging at her lips. "Tristan told me that Sarah meant everything to him. And in that moment, I knew—if I couldn't have him, no one would. That night, I swore I would never let Sarah have the life she took from me."

A silence settled, thick and grim. Eric clenched his fists, torn between rage and heartbreak, as her words continued to cut deeper.

"So, you...you trapped them?" Officer Harris's voice shook with controlled fury.

"Yes," Maya replied simply, her voice filled with a twisted satisfaction. "I wanted them to feel the isolation, the helplessness I felt. I wanted them to see that, no matter where they turned, I would be there, always in control. I put them in that cabin, made sure they couldn't escape. And if they did—well, it would only lead them deeper into my trap."

Eric's face contorted with pain. "Maya, you nearly killed them."

She shrugged, a flicker of guilt crossing her face, only to vanish. "It was either that or let them walk away, believing I was some forgotten memory. I made sure they saw what it was like to be at my mercy, to know that nothing they did would be enough to escape me."

As the weight of her words settled, I looked at Eric, whose gaze was now vacant, pained beyond words. I reached for his hand, hoping that my touch might ground him, and remind him that despite Maya's betrayal, he wasn't alone.

With a chill, I realized Maya's hold over Tristan had never been about love; it had been about control. And she had nearly taken everything from us, all to assert that control. Eric and I, holding tightly to each other, walked out, knowing that though the nightmare was over, the scars of Maya's actions would linger long after.

PART 30 - COFFIN OF NIGHTMARES

The room went still, the air thick with Maya's chilling words.

Officer Harris leaned forward, his voice tight with controlled anger.

"Where are they right now, Maya?" Her expression was serene, almost serene, as if she was sharing a trivial fact.

"In coffins," she replied, her voice eerily calm.

The words hung in the air like a slow-motion horror, pressing down on us with an unbearable weight.

Eric and I shared a look, confusion tightening my chest as I struggled to comprehend her meaning. Before anyone could speak, Maya's voice cut through the silence once more.

"Yes," she repeated, a cold smile creeping onto her face. "In coffins. Buried alive. Beneath my resort."

The floor seemed to tilt beneath me, my pulse roaring in my ears.

I felt Eric's hand tighten around mine, his fingers trembling with fear and rage.

"They were alive last night," Maya continued, the satisfaction in her tone twisting into something monstrous. "But by now..." Her voice trailed off, the unspoken truth slicing through us like a blade.

Eric's face drained of color, and I felt a surge of terror course through me.

We had been upstairs, laughing, sharing moments of happiness—completely oblivious to the fact that Tristan and Sarah were entombed beneath us, fighting for air.

Officer Harris was the first to snap into action. "We have no time to waste!" he barked, motioning for us to move.

"Maya will stay here with the officers. Let's get to the resort. Now."Without another word, we bolted out of the room, Eric and I running side-by-side, the urgency pulsating through our veins.

As we climbed into Eric's car, the realization hit like a punch to the gut—every second mattered.

We tore through the streets, the landscape blurring past, a singular purpose driving us forward.

We reached the resort, and in a heartbeat, we were racing across the grounds, Harris and his team already coordinating the search. Flashlights pierced the dusk, illuminating the vast land around us.

Every second stretched, a torturous reminder that Tristan and Sarah could be slipping further into darkness."Over here!" an officer shouted, pointing to a recently disturbed patch of earth.

With grim efficiency, shovels were brought in, hands working frantically to unearth what lay below. I held my breath, each scrape of metal against dirt like a countdown. Eric was beside me, his face stricken but resolute.

The moment the first edge of the coffin appeared, a surge of desperate hope rose in my chest.

The officers pried it open, and there, pale but breathing, lay Tristan and Sarah. Relief washed over us, the horror momentarily giving way to gratitude.

"We need to get them to the hospital," Harris said, his voice steady but urgent. "Let's see if Sarah and Tristan can make a full recovery. And then...we'll handle Maya."

We nodded, the weight of the ordeal pressing down but a fierce determination propelling us forward. The nightmare wasn't over, but we had them back. And that was the start of a new fight, one we would see through to the very end.

The drive to the hospital was filled with a tense silence, the weight of everything sinking in. The flashing red and blue lights painted the road in vivid colors, but all I could focus on was the sight of Tristan and Sarah in the ambulance, both clinging to life.

Eric's hand gripped mine tightly. I could feel the tremor in his fingers, the raw fear and anger simmering beneath his calm exterior. He looked over at me, his eyes dark with unspoken questions, but neither of us knew what to say. Words felt pointless after what we'd just witnessed.

When we arrived at the hospital, they whisked Tristan and Sarah away to the emergency room, the heavy doors closing with a finality that left us waiting, helpless. Eric and I sank into the cold, hard chairs, our silence weighed down by exhaustion and fear. Theo paced nearby, his gaze fixed on the floor, the lines of worry etched deep into his face.

Minutes stretched into hours, each passing second an agony of anticipation. Maya's betrayal replayed in my mind, the horror of it twisting my stomach. She'd been my best friend, a person I'd shared so many memories with—and yet, none of us had seen this side of her. None of us had sensed the darkness lurking beneath her smile.

Finally, a doctor emerged from the ER, his expression grave yet hopeful. "They're both stable, but it's going to be a long road to recovery. They're lucky you found them when you did."

Relief washed over me, and I sagged back against the chair, my hand gripping Eric's tighter. He exhaled deeply, a shuddering breath that mirrored my own.

"Can we see them?" Theo asked, his voice barely a whisper.

The doctor nodded. "Only for a few minutes. They need rest."

Eric, Theo, and I followed the doctor down the hall, the sterile scent of antiseptic filling the air. When we entered the room, I felt a pang of sorrow seeing Tristan and Sarah lying there, fragile and pale. Machines beeped quietly around them, monitoring their vital signs, while their breaths came in slow, steady rhythms.

I and Eric approached Tristan's bed, feeling the weight of everything I hadn't said, everything I hadn't allowed myself to feel. Theo stood by Sarah, his face a mixture of relief and sadness as he brushed a strand of hair from her forehead.

"Hey, you're safe now," I whispered to Tristan, my voice breaking. "We found you. We're here." said Eric with Sarah.

Tristan's eyes fluttered open, and for a moment, a faint smile played on his lips before he drifted back into sleep.

I glanced at Eric, who looked as if he were carrying the weight of the world on his shoulders. There was a sadness in his eyes, a deep, unspoken grief.

We left the room in silence, allowing Tristan and Sarah to rest. Outside, the weight of reality settled over us. Maya's actions had left scars that ran deeper than anything physical. Eric looked over at me, his gaze filled with a quiet resolve.

As we waited in the hallway, the enormity of what we'd been through began to sink in. The silence was heavy, punctuated only by the faint sounds of the hospital—distant beeps, murmurs, footsteps echoing down the sterile hallways. It was strange to feel this hollow space where anger and betrayal should have been screaming. Instead, there was a numbness, a sort of dazed disbelief at how far Maya had gone.

Eric rested his head in his hands, his fingers threading through his hair as he took a shaky breath.

Theo stood nearby, his arms crossed tightly over his chest as if holding himself together. None of us knew what to say.

Finally, Theo broke the silence. "I still can't believe it... Maya. I mean, sure, she had her moments, but this?" His voice was low, edged with a bitterness that I'd never heard from him before. "She was your best friend, Daisy. She was... everything to all of us at one point. And now..."

He trailed off, looking away as if the words were too painful to complete.

Eric lifted his head, his jaw set with a mix of grief and determination. "She's going to pay for this. I don't care what her reasons were—she crossed a line that can't be uncrossed."

I took a deep breath, feeling a raw ache as memories of Maya drifted through my mind. How many times had I trusted her? How many times had I poured my heart out to her, believing she was my confidante, my sister in everything that mattered? Yet none of that had stopped her from hurting the people closest to me.

A pair of officers approached us, one of them Officer Harris, the gravity in his eyes unmistakable.

"We're transferring Maya to a more secure facility. Her actions... well, it's clear she poses a significant threat to others." He hesitated, glancing at each of us. "We need a full statement from all of you. The DA wants to ensure there are no loose ends."

Theo nodded, the hint of resentment flickering across his face. "Let's get it over with. She deserves nothing from us now."

Eric glanced back toward the hospital room doors, his expression a mixture of pain and anger.

"Let's make sure our statement covers everything," he said quietly. "Every detail. She deserves to be held accountable in every possible way."

We were led to a small room down the hall, and Officer Harris waited for us to sit before he started asking questions. With every answer we gave, it felt like we were unraveling the story of a stranger—not the Maya we'd known, but the twisted person she had become. Each detail we shared deepened the wound, making the betrayal feel fresher, sharper. It was like reopening an injury we hadn't realized was still bleeding.

When we were finished, Harris closed his notebook, his gaze lingering on us. "I can't begin to imagine what this has been like for you," he said. "But you did the right thing by coming forward and helping us understand Maya's intentions. We'll handle this now."

We nodded numbly, exhaustion pulling us down like a weight. As we stood to leave, Harris held up a hand, his expression serious. "Just one more thing—there's a chance she'll go to trial for this, and if she does, you might be asked to testify."

The reality of it all hit us anew, the gravity of everything pressing down on us. It was no longer just a horrific event we could distance ourselves from; it was something we'd be tied to, called upon to relive, over and over.

But as we left the hospital that night, the weight of what had happened only strengthened our resolve. Maya had destroyed every bond we'd had with her, severed every tie, but she'd also united us in a way we hadn't anticipated. Now, we were bound not by friendship or shared history but by a shared purpose—a promise to seek justice for those she'd hurt and to make sure her betrayal never found new victims.

In the car, Eric reached for my hand, his fingers warm against mine. "Whatever happens next, we're in this together," he said, his voice soft but firm. I looked over at Theo, who gave me a silent nod of agreement. And in that moment, I knew that whatever lay ahead, we'd face it together.

Part 31 - Fractured Echoes

As I watched Eric, his shoulders shaking, a knot formed in my throat. I had never seen him like this—his usual calm, steady presence shattered, replaced by a vulnerability that felt both foreign and heartbreaking.

Red-rimmed eyes filled with unshed tears, as though he were willing the universe to change what had happened to his sister.

In that moment, he seemed almost fragile, a side of Eric that was rare, almost feminine in its tenderness. Seeing him like this made my heart ache with a new kind of pain, an empathy so deep it felt woven into my very being. I took a hesitant step closer, wanting to reach out, to do something, but he closed his eyes, turning slightly away as if bracing himself.

Theo put a gentle hand on my shoulder, his expression shadowed with a quiet understanding. Eric turned to us, his voice hoarse as he spoke.

"Theo, please...take Daisy home," he murmured, his tone a mix of exhaustion and resolve. "You get home safe too. I... I need to be here, to stay with my parents through this. They shouldn't be alone right now."

My eyes met his, but there was nothing I could say to bridge the chasm of sorrow between us. I felt my heart fracture a little at the sight of him—his strength folded in on itself, his pain spilling over in ways I had never imagined. It felt almost unbearable, as though his grief had somehow become my own.

Theo nodded, his voice soft. "Of course. I'll make sure Daisy gets home safe."

Eric's gaze lingered on me for a moment, searching for something unspoken. And as Theo gently led me away, I stole one last look at Eric, wishing that I could somehow carry some of his pain, even if just for a moment.

As Theo drove, the quiet hum of the engine filled the silence between us. He finally spoke, his voice gentle, as if unveiling pieces of the past he'd held onto.

"You know, Tristan was never a cheater, Daisy. He... he just didn't know how to take care of you. He was always caught up in what he thought you should be rather than who you were."

Theo glanced at me, the weight of his words hanging heavy. "There were times when he'd judge you for the very things that made you come alive, like your passion and your social world. It was sad because, even when he wasn't fully there for you, he knew he was hurting you."

Theo paused, his gaze distant, as though reaching back to a memory. "Once, he told me, 'I hurt her, Theo. Our relationship...it was a beautiful disaster. We tried, but we could never find our rhythm together.' I felt his regret, Daisy. It was deep and real."

"Some stories are meant to teach us, not complete us, and sometimes, losing something that couldn't hold us is the first step to finding the one who will."

After a moment, Theo's expression softened, and a faint smile tugged at his lips. "Then Sarah came into his life, and everything shifted. They fit, as if all those rough edges had smoothed out."

He looked at me, his eyes warm. "And, you know, I always thought you'd find someone better, someone who would see you for everything you are."

He paused, his gaze steady, and then he said, "And here he is—Eric. He's the one, Daisy. I've never been more sure."

"Sometimes the love we think we want is only a shadow, while the one we need is standing right beside us, rousing every dimmed part of our soul."

As we pulled up to my house, Theo put the car in park, glancing at me with a mix of concern and encouragement. I managed a small smile, knowing he'd been there for me every step of the way.

"Thank you, Theo. For...everything," I murmured. He simply nodded, his eyes soft as he watched me head toward the house.

The door opened before I even reached it, and my mom rushed out, her arms wrapping around me tightly. I could feel the quiet worry in her embrace, the unspoken relief that I was home, safe.

She pulled back just enough to look at me, her eyes glistening. "We know, honey. About everything. This...this is a lot for anyone to go through, especially you."

Behind her, my dad approached, his gaze steady but filled with a quiet strength. He placed a comforting hand on my back, his voice warm and reassuring. "Sometimes, you have to lose yourself to find where you truly belong."

"Remember, no storm lasts forever honey. You may get swept up in its clutter, but it's the calm you find afterward that shows you where you're meant to be."

I turned back to wave at Theo, my parents joining with a soft wave of their own as he nodded in return, a silent promise hanging in the air that this wasn't goodbye—just another part of our journey.

Once Theo drove away, I felt the weight of silence around me, the intensity of everything that had happened finally settling in. My mom guided me inside, her arm wrapped protectively around my shoulders. The familiar warmth of our home felt like a balm, but beneath it was a heaviness that wouldn't be easy to shake.

I sank onto the couch, and my mom sat beside me, brushing a stray strand of hair from my face as she studied me. "Sweetheart, you don't have to explain everything right now. But...if there's anything you need, we're here. Both of us."

I looked up to see my dad nodding, his quiet presence offering a steady comfort. The worry etched in his face softened as he took a seat across from me. He opened his mouth, hesitated, then spoke, his voice carrying a depth that I hadn't expected.

"Daisy, life has a way of giving us the hardest lessons in the most unexpected ways. Sometimes, it's through people we thought we knew, and sometimes, it's through ourselves. I know this might not make sense right now, but everything you've experienced will shape you into someone even stronger."

The warmth of their words wrapped around me, and for a moment, I let myself lean into it, absorbing their support.

Later that evening, I found myself back in my room, a soft glow from my lamp casting gentle shadows on the walls. I pulled out my Artsy Diary, fingers tracing over the worn cover, and let my mind drift. Maya, Tristan, Sarah, Theo, Eric...all of them had woven themselves so intricately into this story that had started out so differently than where it was now.

I thought back to Theo's words on the ride home, about how Tristan hadn't known how to take care of me and how he had regretted the things he'd done. It struck me as bittersweet—a reminder of a chapter I'd closed but one that had still shaped me, just as my dad had said.

I opened my notebook to a fresh page and began to write, letting the words flow freely.

"To those who are pieces of my story,

the ones who added weight to my pages and the ones who made them lighter. There was a time when I thought we'd be bound together in ink, yet some of us drifted, and others stayed. But each mark, each memory, is a part of who I am. And somewhere within, I found myself, more powerful for what was left behind."

The quietness of my room felt less empty now, filled instead with a peace that had long eluded me. And as I set my pen down, I knew that, no matter what happened next, I had begun to make peace with this tangled story.

PART 32 - IN THE WAKE OF ANGER

The next few days were a whirlwind of emotions and changes, each moment feeling like a delicate balancing act. As news of Maya's actions spread, the community buzzed with shock and disbelief. I found it hard to comprehend the depths of her betrayal, especially when we had shared so many memories together.

School felt surreal. I walked through the halls, the whispers of my classmates trailing behind me like shadows. Everyone seemed to know the story, speculating about what had happened and how Maya could have done such terrible things. I was grateful for the support of my friends—Eric and Theo were my anchors amidst the storm, but even their presence couldn't shield me from the weight of it all.

One afternoon, I found myself sitting on a bench outside, staring blankly at the schoolyard. The air was warm, but a chill ran through me as I thought about Sarah and Tristan still recovering in the hospital. They had been through so much, and I felt a heaviness in my chest thinking about their pain.

"Hey, you okay?" Theo's voice broke through my thoughts, and I turned to see him approaching. He sat down beside me, concern etched in his features.

"I don't know, Theo. I just can't wrap my head around everything. How could Maya do that? I thought we were friends." I buried my face in my hands, overwhelmed by a sense of loss for the friendship I had once cherished.

Theo leaned in, his presence warm and steady. "It's okay to feel this way. Sometimes, people surprise us in the evilest ways. But you can't blame yourself for her steps, Daisy. You were never responsible for what she chose to do."

I nodded, taking a deep breath. "I know, but I can't shake this feeling. It's like a part of me is grieving not just for Sarah and Tristan, but for the friendship I thought we had."

Theo paused, considering his words. "Friendships change, especially when people show their true colors. It's hard, but it's also a part of growing up. You'll find those who are worthy of your trust."

Just then, Eric joined us, his expression more solemn than usual. "I just heard from the hospital. Sarah's awake, and she's asking for you, Daisy."

My heart raced, a mix of relief and anxiety coursing through me. "Really? Is Tristan okay?"

"They're both stable, but Sarah needs her friends right now. It's time to go see her." Eric's voice was firm, but I could see the sadness in his eyes, reflecting the gravity of the situation.

As we made our way to the hospital, I couldn't help but feel a sense of dread. What would Sarah say? How would she feel seeing me after everything that had happened? My heart pounded in my chest as we entered the hospital, the antiseptic smell hitting me like a wave.

In the room, Sarah lay propped up in bed, her face pale but her spirit strong. When she saw me, her eyes lit up, and I felt a rush of emotion flood through me.

"Daisy!" she exclaimed, her voice weak but filled with relief. "I'm so glad you're here."

I rushed to her side, tears pricking at the corners of my eyes. "I'm so sorry, Sarah. I can't believe what happened. Are you okay?"

She nodded, though it was evident she was still shaken. "I've been better, but I'll be okay. I just... I don't understand why Maya would do this to us."

I squeezed her hand, feeling the warmth and connection between us despite everything.

As we sat there, I saw Eric and Theo exchanging glances, silently acknowledging the weight of the moment. We were all grappling with the aftermath of Maya's actions, but in that room, there was a glimmer of hope. We would support each other through the darkness and help Sarah find her way back to the light.

After a long conversation filled with shared memories and unspoken fears, Sarah took a deep breath. "You know, even though this has been the worst experience of my life, I can't help but feel grateful for you guys. You've been here when I needed you the most."

I smiled through my tears, my heart swelling with gratitude for the friendships that remained intact amidst the chaos.

"We're family, Sarah. No matter what, we'll always be here for each other."

As the evening wore on, laughter slowly replaced the sadness. We recounted funny stories from our past, trying to distract ourselves from the reality that loomed over us. I realized that while Maya had tried to tear us apart, the bonds of our friendship had only grown stronger through adversity.

When it was time to leave, I hugged Sarah tightly, promising her I'd be back soon. "You're going to be okay. I believe in you."

With renewed determination, I stepped out of the hospital.

That night, I lay in bed, staring at the ceiling as my thoughts spiraled. The moonlight filtered through the curtains, casting soft shadows that danced across the room. I couldn't shake the feeling that I needed to see Maya, to confront her directly and understand what had driven her to such a dark place. Eric and Theo were against it, but I felt a pull, a need to find closure amidst the chaos she had created.

"Daisy, you really don't have to do this," Eric said, his voice filled with concern as we sat together on my bed. "Maya made her choices, and you don't owe her anything."

"I know, but I just want to hear it from her," I replied, my voice barely above a whisper. "I need to understand why she did what she did, even if it hurts. Just once, I want to look her in the eye and see if there's any remorse."

Theo glanced at Eric, then back at me. "If you really want to do this, we'll go with you tomorrow. But promise us you'll be careful."

"Promise," I said, a mixture of determination and dread swirling within me.

As the night wore on, I felt a heavy weight in my chest, an anticipation mixed with anxiety. What would I say to her? Would she even acknowledge the pain she had caused? My mind raced, turning over every possible scenario until exhaustion finally claimed me.

The next morning, Theo and Eric arrived at my house, their faces serious. They had spoken to my parents before coming up, and as I joined them downstairs, I noticed the tension in the air.

"Daisy," my mom said, her eyes soft but firm. "Are you sure about this? You don't have to go see her."

"She needs to understand what she did," I insisted, meeting her gaze. "I just want to know why."

Dad stood behind her, crossing his arms, his expression unreadable. "If you feel this strongly, we won't stop you. But we want you to be safe."

I nodded, grateful for their support despite the circumstances. Eric and Theo exchanged glances, and then we headed out, the car ride filled with a tense silence, each of us lost in our thoughts.

Arriving at the prison felt surreal. The gray concrete walls loomed above us, cold and unwelcoming. After a quick check-in with the officers, they led us to a small room with a one-way mirror, where I would see Maya through a glass barrier. My heart raced as the door opened, and I caught my first glimpse of her.

Maya entered, her expression flat, almost indifferent. She didn't look sad or guilty; instead, her face seemed to say, "Why would you come to see me?"

"Why am I here, Maya?" I asked, my voice trembling slightly. "What were you thinking?"

She leaned back, crossing her arms defiantly. "What do you think? I didn't ask you to come here."

Eric placed a hand on my shoulder, a silent reminder to stay calm. "Daisy, we don't need to do this. Let's go."

Maya shot Eric a bitchy look, her eyes narrowing as she crossed her arms. But I shook my head. "Just give me a moment, please."

But I shook my head. "Just give me a moment, please."

Eric hesitated, but Theo nodded in agreement. "We'll wait outside."

As they left the room, Maya looked around, her expression shifting slightly as if she were taking in the reality of her situation. "I'm sorry," she finally said, the words barely a whisper, a flicker of shame passing over her features.

My heart sank. Maybe there was a chance for redemption, a glimpse of the friend I once knew. "Maya, you don't have to—"

But before I could finish, she interrupted, her voice rising with anger. "Did you think I would say that? Bitch, never! Just get lost from my sight!"

She turned away, her anger cutting deeper than I expected. I felt my breath hitch, the tears welling up despite my best efforts to hold them back. I had hoped for understanding, for even a hint of remorse, but all I found was bitterness.

The officers nearby noticed the commotion and approached. "She's been going through some serious mental struggles," one officer said gently. "We have therapists working with her daily, but it's tough. She may change eventually, but right now, she's struggling."

I stepped outside, my heart heavy with confusion and sorrow. As I reached the waiting area, I spotted Theo and Eric running toward me, their concern evident.

"What happened?" Theo asked, worry etched across his face.

I wiped my eyes, fighting to keep my composure. "Nothing. I just... I didn't get what I wanted. She's still angry. She doesn't care."

Eric pulled me into a hug, his warmth wrapping around me like a lifeline. "You did what you needed to do, Daisy. You faced her. That takes strength."

"But it didn't help," I said, my voice shaky. "I thought maybe... maybe there was a chance to understand her, to see if she felt anything. But all I got was anger."

"Sometimes people can't show remorse, especially when they're lost in their own pain," Theo said gently. "You tried, and that's what matters."

As we walked away from the prison, I couldn't shake the feeling of loss. I had hoped for closure, but instead, I was left with more questions than answers. The weight of betrayal hung heavy in the air, but I knew I had friends by my side, and together, we would navigate the aftermath of this haunting experience.

PART 33 - FINDING LIGHT TOGETHER

As we walked away from the prison, the tension in the air lingered like a heavy fog. Theo's phone buzzed, and he glanced at the screen, his brow furrowing. "I have to take this," he said, stepping aside to answer the call. I could hear the low murmur of his voice as he spoke to his dad, but it felt distant, as if I were underwater.

Eric stood beside me, the weight of the day pressing on both of us. After a few moments, Theo hung up, running a hand through his hair. "I had some work with my dad," he said, his tone apologetic. "I need to leave."

"Are you okay?" I asked, concern etching my voice. I didn't want him to feel like he had to leave when we all needed each other right now.

"Yeah, I'll be fine. Just... you know how it is. I'll check in later, okay?" He gave me a reassuring smile, but it didn't quite reach his eyes. I nodded, grateful for his support, even if it was brief.Once Theo walked away, I turned to Eric, who was watching me intently. "You okay?" he asked, his voice low and soothing.

"Yeah, just a lot to process," I replied. "It feels like everything is unraveling, and I'm just... lost.""Let's go somewhere quiet," he suggested, his hand slipping into mine. "Somewhere we can talk without all the noise."

I nodded, feeling the warmth of his grip envelop my worries, and we began to walk farther away from the city. The streets grew quieter, the hustle and bustle fading into a serene stillness. Eventually, we found a secluded park, where the trees whispered above us, casting dappled shadows on the ground.

As we settled onto a bench beneath the canopy of leaves, Eric looked at me thoughtfully. "Darling," he said, his voice almost a whisper, "Do you know what I would tell my daughter when she becomes a teenager?"

I leaned in, intrigued by his words. "What would you say?"

He took a deep breath, his gaze softening. "I'd say, 'Go into a relationship only when you truly understand what love is.' Your mom and I, we're an example of that. And if you find someone like me, just go love him. But remember, love is beautiful, but it can also hurt."

As he spoke, I felt a pang in my chest, realizing that while a boy might leave and come back, thinking only one chapter of their story was affected, when a girl leaves, it means she reconsiders the entire narrative of their shared history and the future that could have been. My heart swelled at his words, the vulnerability of the moment washing over me. "That's wise advice."

I looked into Eric's eyes, searching for the kindness and understanding I had come to rely on. "Do you really believe that?"

"I do," he said softly. "It's all about understanding yourself and knowing your worth. And I want you to know your worth, Daisy."

A lump formed in my throat, the weight of his affection overwhelming me. "Thank you, Eric. For everything."

He smiled, that comforting warmth radiating between us. "You don't have to thank me. I'm here for you, no matter what. Always."

In that peaceful moment, I realized how much I needed this conversation, how Eric's presence was like a beacon guiding me through the storm. As we sat there, hands intertwined, I felt a flicker of hope igniting within me, a promise of brighter days ahead, despite the shadows that lingered in my heart.

I took a deep breath, my heart heavy with the weight of my words. "But Eric, even I wasn't good enough. I pushed Tristan away when all I wanted was to not talk to him in that moment. I thought that would protect me, but it only made things worse."

Eric turned to face me fully, his expression a mix of concern and compassion. "Daisy, you were never the problem. You were just trying to protect yourself from getting hurt. It's natural to feel overwhelmed and want to retreat into yourself."

"But I should've fought for him," I said, my voice cracking. "Instead, I shut him out. I thought that by creating distance, I could shield myself from pain. All I did was build a wall, and now... now I'm left wondering if I lost him forever because of it."

Eric shook his head, frustration flickering in his eyes. "You're not responsible for how he reacted. You can't control someone else's feelings or actions. You were in a difficult place, and you were trying to cope the best way you knew how. Sometimes, that means stepping back. You are human, Daisy."

"I just wish I had done things differently," I confessed, feeling the tears brimming in my eyes. "I wish I could go back and change everything."

"That's the thing about life, isn't it?" Eric replied softly, brushing a strand of hair behind my ear.

"We can't change the past, but we can learn from it. Every experience, every heartbreak, it shapes us into who we are. It's painful, but it's part of the journey."

I nodded, the tears spilling down my cheeks. "It hurts so much, Eric. I feel so lost, like I'm trapped in this cycle of regret and confusion."

He wrapped an arm around my shoulders, pulling me close. "You're not alone in this. I'm here for you, and I always will be. You can take your time to heal, and you don't have to rush into anything. Just remember, you are worth so much more than you realize."

His words wrapped around me like a warm blanket, offering comfort in the midst of my storm.

"Thank you, Eric. For being patient with me and for understanding."

"Always," he replied, his voice a gentle promise. "And you don't have to be perfect to be loved. You're allowed to be messy and vulnerable. It's what makes you real."

I leaned against him, finding solace in his presence. The night felt less daunting with him by my side. "I just hope I can find a way to forgive myself one day."

"Start small," he encouraged, squeezing my hand. "Forgiveness isn't a destination; it's a journey. It takes time, and that's okay. Just take it one step at a time, and I'll be right here with you."

As I closed my eyes, resting my head against his shoulder, I felt a flicker of hope igniting within me. Maybe I could find a way to forgive myself. With Eric beside me, I knew I didn't have to navigate this path alone. Together, we could face whatever came next.

"And look, Tristan said he would never go into another relationship after we broke up," I said, my voice trembling with frustration. "He promised me that!"

Eric's brow furrowed slightly as he processed my words. "Daisy, do you think that's betrayal? I mean, he's with Sarah now. It might look like he broke that promise, but maybe it's not as black and white as it seems."

"What do you mean?" I asked, confused.

He took a deep breath, searching for the right words. "Sometimes, when people say they won't date anyone else, they're just trying to cope with the pain of a breakup. Tristan might have meant it in that moment, but as time went on, he might've realized he was ready to find love again. It doesn't negate what you two shared; it just means he found a different path."

"But it still feels like a betrayal," I replied, feeling the ache in my chest deepen. "How could he move on so easily?"

"Moving on doesn't mean he didn't care about you," Eric explained gently. "It's complicated. He might have needed time to figure things out, and sometimes that involves connecting with someone new. It doesn't erase your history together."

I thought about his words, trying to grasp the nuance of what he was saying. "So, you think it's possible for him to find love again without it being a betrayal to what we had?"

"Absolutely," Eric affirmed, his eyes locking onto mine with a fierce intensity. "Love is not finite. It doesn't diminish because of someone else. It can grow and evolve. Maybe Tristan just needed to rediscover what love felt like, and it took him finding it in Sarah to realize that."

I sighed, the weight of my emotions washing over me. "I want to believe that. I really do. But it's hard to separate my feelings of hurt from the reality of what he's experiencing now."

"Of course, it's hard," Eric said, his voice filled with empathy. "Your feelings are valid. But don't let those feelings blind you to the possibility that he's on his own journey, just like you are. It's okay to be hurt, but don't let that hurt consume you. It's part of the healing process."

His words hung in the air, a bittersweet reminder of the complexities of love and loss. "So, what do I do now?" I asked, feeling lost in the fog of my emotions.

"Take your time to heal," he replied firmly. "Reflect on what you've learned from this experience, and know that it's okay to feel a mix of emotions. Just remember, moving forward doesn't mean forgetting; it means honoring your past while embracing what's next."

I smiled weakly, appreciating the wisdom he offered. "Thank you for helping me see things differently. I guess it's just going to take time for me to process everything."

"Time is the most important part," Eric said softly, brushing a tear from my cheek with his thumb. "And I'll be right here, every step of the way. You're not alone in this."

As we stood together, the weight of the world felt a little lighter. Maybe there was hope for me yet, and with Eric by my side, I could begin to navigate this tangled web of emotions with a clearer heart.

"Do you think I'm being too forward about our relationship?" I asked, my voice barely above a whisper. Doubt gnawed at me, twisting my stomach into knots. "I just feel like I shouldn't be in love unless I heal first. I don't want to hurt you."

Eric's expression softened, and he took a step closer, bridging the gap between us. "Daisy, it's completely natural to feel that way, especially after everything you've been through. But I want you to know that you're not alone in this. I'm here for you, every step of the way."

"But what if I bring my baggage into this?" I pressed, feeling vulnerable and exposed. "What if I can't fully let go of my past?"

He shook his head gently, his eyes filled with warmth and understanding. "We all carry our baggage, but that doesn't mean we can't find love along the way. You don't have to have everything figured out to open your heart again. Love is a journey, and it's okay to take that journey together, even when it's messy."

"But I don't want to drag you into my pain," I said, my voice trembling with uncertainty. "I don't want to hurt you because I'm not fully healed."

"Listen to me," Eric said, his tone firm yet soothing. "I would take care of that, my princess. I would heal you with my love. You don't have to worry about that. Love is about support and understanding. It's about being there for each other when things get tough."

Tears welled in my eyes at his words, feeling both relieved and overwhelmed. "You make it sound so easy, but I don't want to be a burden."

"You could never be a burden to me," he replied, his voice steady and reassuring. "You're my priority, and I want to help you find your way back to yourself. We can face this together, and I promise to be patient. You don't have to rush into any-thing. Just take your time."

I nodded, feeling a mix of hope and fear. "What if I'm not ready for this? What if I end up hurting you more in the end?"

He reached out and cupped my face in his hands, his gaze steady and unwavering. "You won't know unless you try. And if it gets tough, we'll tackle it together. I'll be here to catch you when you fall, and I'll help you stand back up again. That's what love is about—being there through the highs and the lows."

His words settled into my heart, soothing my worries like a gentle balm. I could feel the warmth radiating from him, a promise of safety and care. Maybe, just maybe, I could allow myself to take this leap.

"I'm scared," I confessed, my voice trembling.

"I know," Eric said softly. "But I'll be right here with you, holding your hand every step of the way. You're not alone, and you don't have to face your fears by yourself."

In that moment, I realized that maybe I could allow myself to love again. With Eric by my side, I felt a flicker of hope ignite within me—a hope that whispered of healing and new beginnings. I took a deep breath, allowing his words to wash over me, filling the empty spaces in my heart with the promise of a brighter tomorrow.

Part 34 - When Hearts Align

As the sun dipped below the horizon, painting the sky in warm hues of amber and rose, Eric and I sat close, savoring the quiet comfort between us. The soft orange light cast shadows around us, making everything feel surreal, as if we were the only two people left in the world.

Just as I started to get lost in the moment, my phone pinged, breaking the stillness. I glanced down and saw a text from my mom: "It's sun downing. Come home quick."

I sighed, the spell of tranquility slipping away, and turned to Eric. "Looks like my mom's calling me home," I said, showing him the message with a half-smile.

He chuckled softly, brushing a stray lock of hair from my face. "Alright, princess," he said, his voice tender. "Let's get you home before the sun completely disappears on us."

We climbed back into his car, and as he drove, silence fell between us. It wasn't an uncomfortable silence, though. Instead, it felt like we were both soaking up the remnants of the evening, carrying the peace of it forward with us.

As we pulled up to my house, I could see my parents watching from the living room window, their silhouettes framed by the glow of the lights inside. I turned to Eric, hesitating for a moment, not quite ready to say goodbye.

"Thank you, Eric," I said softly, searching his face. "For everything."

He smiled, reaching over to squeeze my hand. "Anytime, Daisy. You don't have to thank me. Just... take care of yourself tonight, alright?"

I nodded, giving his hand one last squeeze before letting go and stepping out of the car. As I walked toward the house, I heard him call out, "Goodnight."

"Goodnight," I replied, turning back to wave as he pulled away, his car disappearing into the darkening street.

I felt my parents' eyes on me as I walked in, my mom reaching out to pull me into a hug. "Glad you're home," she whispered. My dad offered me a gentle pat on the back, his way of saying he cared, even without words.

Turning back, I caught one last glimpse of Eric's taillights vanishing into the night, carrying with them the lingering warmth of our shared sunset.

At dinner, I sat across from my parents, feeling the quiet buzz of the day still humming within me.

The warm, familiar smells of my mom's cooking filled the room, grounding me in a way that I hadn't realized I needed. My parents exchanged a few glances, each one laced with curiosity, until finally, my dad cleared his throat and looked at me.

"So," he started, carefully, "we saw Eric dropped you off earlier."

I knew this was my moment, and for the first time, I didn't feel a hint of fear or hesitation. Looking at them both, I spoke, feeling the words come naturally, like a breath of fresh air. "I love him, Mom, Dad. We're together. Eric and I."

There was a pause, but it wasn't filled with tension. Instead, it felt like something warm and gentle unfolding. My mom's face softened, her eyes lighting up with something between relief and happiness. "Oh, honey," she said, reaching across the table to take my hand, "we're happy for you. Truly."

My dad nodded, giving a small, approving smile. "I've seen how he looks at you," he said, his tone quiet but steady. "He's a good man. And we can see that he cares about you."

Hearing them say that filled me with a weightless joy, like a part of me had been set free.

Dinner continued, but I felt more at ease than I had in ages, like everything had fallen perfectly into place.

Later that night, as I settled into my room, I felt a sense of calm I hadn't felt in a long time. My parents' acceptance of Eric felt like a cornerstone, anchoring everything that had been uncertain in my life.

I leaned back against the pillows, scrolling absentmindedly through my phone, until a notification popped up on my screen.

It was a new post from Sarah.

I hesitated for a moment, my finger hovering over the notification, before I opened it. The image was from the day we'd visited Tristan and Sarah at the hospital—a candid shot of all of us.

Tristan was sitting up in the hospital bed, his arm slung protectively around Sarah's shoulders. Eric and Theo stood beside me, our expressions warm but tired.

The caption read:

"Some moments change us. Not always in ways we expect, but sometimes in ways we need. Healing isn't a straight line, but it's easier when you have the right people by your side. Here's to second chances and finding the strength to start over."

I stared at the post, letting her words sink in. There was no bitterness in me anymore when I looked at Tristan with Sarah. It felt like looking at an old photograph—familiar, but distant, like a life that belonged to someone else.

A message from Eric lit up my screen:

"Hey, princess. Saw Sarah's post. Made me think about how far we've all come. Proud of you. Sleep well, my love."

I smiled at his words, the warmth of them curling around me like a blanket. I typed back: "Thank you, Eric. For everything. Sleep well too."

As I set my phone aside, I felt a quiet contentment settle over me. The day had started with weight and uncertainty but had ended with clarity and love.

I turned off the light and lay back, watching the moonlight spill across the walls of my room. Life was far from perfect, but for the first time, it felt like it was mine to rebuild—on my terms, with the people I chose to keep by my side.

Eric's words echoed softly in my mind, a steady reassurance: "Some things end to make space for something better."

As the house settled into the quiet of the night, I curled up under my blanket, ready to let sleep take over. But a nagging thought tugged at me, refusing to let me drift off.

I suddenly remembered—I hadn't written in my Artsy Diary, the one place where I poured out pieces of myself. It had been my anchor through every storm, and tonight felt too important to leave unwritten.

I swung my legs off the bed and padded over to my desk, flipping open the soft, worn cover of the diary. My fingers automatically reached for the pen tucked neatly inside.

The date came first, inscribed carefully in the top corner, just as I always did. My mind lingered for a moment, replaying the sunset, Eric's tender words, and my parents' acceptance. Then, smiling softly, I reached for a small printed sticker from my collection, a habit I'd recently started to mark moments that felt different—moments that felt monumental. This one read: "Growth is messy, but it's mine to cherish."

I peeled the backing carefully and pressed the sticker onto the page, its bold but graceful font sitting snugly in the corner. It felt fitting, like the perfect reminder of the day's small triumphs—the conversations that had peeled away another layer of fear and uncertainty.

With the sticker in place, I let the words flow: "Today felt like a breath I've been holding for years. Eric made me feel seen, truly seen, in a way I didn't think possible. And my parents... their acceptance was like walking into sunlight after a long storm. I'm scared to hope, but maybe, just maybe, things can be okay."

I paused, staring at the fresh ink against the pale page. It didn't feel complete.

Biting my lip, I added one more line, whispering the words aloud as I wrote:

"Even if love is uncertain, it's still worth believing in."

Satisfied, I closed the diary with a sense of finality, placing it back in its special spot on my desk. As I slid back under my blanket, a calm settled over me, and for the first time in a while, sleep came easily.

PART 35 - THE FINAL WORD

To my cherished readers,

As I sit down to write this, I feel a strange mix of emotions—gratitude, nostalgia, and a quiet kind of vulnerability. Bringing this story to life has been a journey, one that mirrored parts of my own life in ways I never expected. Every word, every moment, every heartbreak, and every triumph felt like a tiny piece of my soul shared with you.

Love is one of those things we think we understand until it surprises us. It's not just the flutter in your chest or the warmth in someone's gaze. It's messy. It's a tangled web of emotions, sacrifices, misunderstandings, and second chances. Sometimes, it feels like holding onto a storm, desperately hoping the winds will calm. Other times, it feels like the safest harbor you've ever known.

This story isn't just about romantic love. It's about the love between friends, the love within families, and most importantly, the love we learn to give ourselves. It's about finding beauty in the brokenness and hope in the things we never thought we'd survive.

As you read, maybe you saw a reflection of yourself in the characters. Maybe you saw your past or glimpses of your future. Maybe it reminded you of someone you once loved—or someone you still do. Whatever it was, I hope it reminded you of this: you are not alone.

There was a time in my life when I thought I had to have everything figured out. I thought love was supposed to be simple, that relationships were meant to complete us, and that life had a clear, straight path forward. But life, as it turns out, is far more unpredictable than that. It's in the detours where we find our most defining moments.

To love someone—truly, deeply—is to take a risk. It's to open yourself up to the possibility of heartbreak but also to the beauty of connection. I've learned that love doesn't require perfection. It asks for patience, understanding, and the courage to show up even when it's hard. This story, in many ways, was my way of processing those lessons. The moments of doubt, the unexpected betrayals, the quiet joys, and the bittersweet endings—all of it was a reflection of things I've felt or seen or imagined.

There was a night, not too long ago, when I found myself staring at an empty page, unsure if I could continue writing. I wondered if my words mattered if they could truly reach anyone. And then I thought of you—someone out there, reading these very words. I imagined you finding comfort, clarity, or even just a moment of escape in this story. That thought gave me the strength to keep going.

We often talk about closure, about the idea of neatly tying up loose ends and moving on. But I've come to realize that life rarely offers such clean endings. Instead, we learn to carry the unresolved parts with us, letting them shape us without letting them define us. It's in that delicate balance that we find peace.

For me, writing has always been about connection. It's about taking the swirling chaos inside my heart and putting it into words that someone else might understand. It's about saying, "Hey, I've felt this too," and hoping it resonates with someone on the other side of the page.

As I look back on this story, I think about all the characters—their flaws, their fears, their quiet moments of courage. Each of them taught me something. Daisy reminded me of the importance of staying true to myself, even when it's scary. Eric showed me what it means to love without conditions, to be someone's safe place. Maya, complicated as she was, reminded me that pain can twist us in ways we don't always recognize, but healing is always possible. And Theo, with his steady presence, was a reminder that sometimes the people we least expect can surprise us the most.

I don't know where you are right now as you read this. Maybe you're curled up in bed with a cup of tea, or maybe you're on a crowded train, stealing a few moments for yourself. Wherever you are, I want you to know how much it means to me that you're here, sharing this journey with me. If there's one thing I hope you take away from this story, it's this: You are enough. Your scars, your fears, your dreams—they all make you who you are. And who you are is worthy of love, respect, and joy.

Life doesn't always go as we plan. Relationships don't always last. People don't always stay. But even in the midst of loss and uncertainty, there is beauty to be found. There are sunsets that take your breath away, laughter that heals old wounds, and love that surprises you when you least expect it.

So here's my promise to you, dear reader: No matter what you're facing, there is light ahead. It may not come in the way you expect, but it will come. Hold onto hope. Hold onto the people who make you feel seen. And never stop believing in your own strength.

As I close this chapter, I do so with a heart full of gratitude. Thank you for letting me share this story with you. Thank you for giving my words a home. And thank you for being part of this journey. Until we meet again, With love and endless gratitude, Daisy.